Pokémon

SWORD & SHIELD

2

STORY
Hidenori Kusaka

ART
Satoshi Yamamoto

Henry
SWORD

HENRY IS A CRAFTSMAN WHO UNDERSTANDS POKÉMON GEAR. HE IS THE DESCENDANT OF A RENOWNED SWORDSMITH AND USES FAMILY SECRETS TO ENHANCE THE GEAR HE COMES ACROSS.

Casey
SHIELD

CASEY IS AN ACE COMPUTER HACKER WHO CAN CRACK ANY CODE AND GUESS ANY PASSWORD. SHE'S PROFESSOR MAGNOLIA'S ASSISTANT AND CHIPS IN AS THE TEAM'S DATA ANALYST.

Character Introduction

Marvin

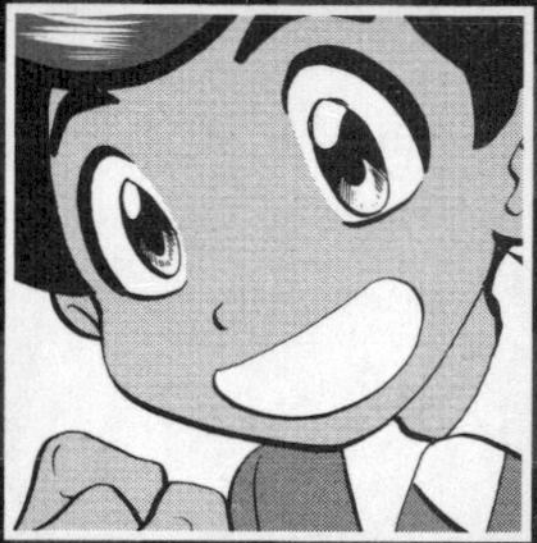

MARVIN'S A ROOKIE TRAINER WHO RECENTLY MOVED TO GALAR. HE'S EXCITED TO LEARN EVERYTHING HE CAN ABOUT POKÉMON!

Professor Magnolia

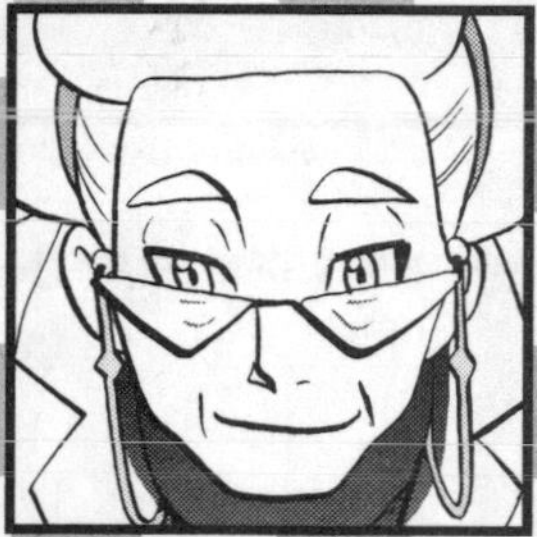

Leon

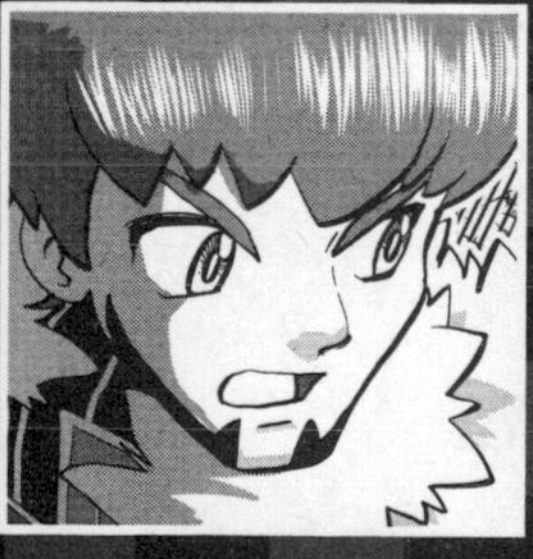

LEON IS THE BEST TRAINER IN GALAR. HE'S THE UNDEFEATED CHAMPION!

Sonia

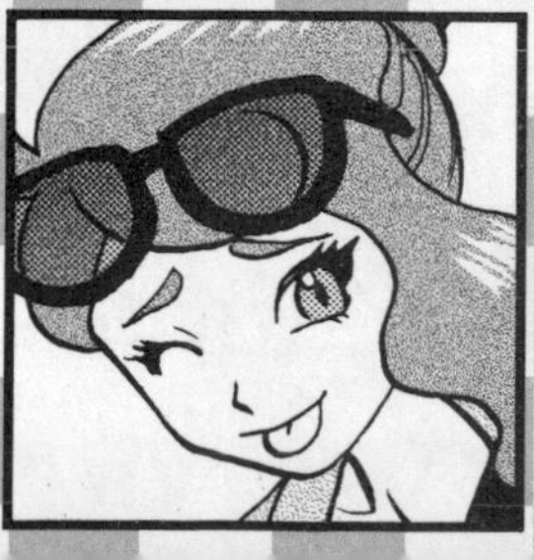

SONIA IS PROFESSOR MAGNOLIA'S GRANDDAUGHTER AND LEON'S CHILDHOOD FRIEND. SHE SETS OUT TO INVESTIGATE THE GALAR REGION LEGEND AFTER BEING PROMPTED TO DO SO BY PROFESSOR MAGNOLIA.

CONTENTS

Adventure 5 Ooh, Shiny!! Legendary Equipment

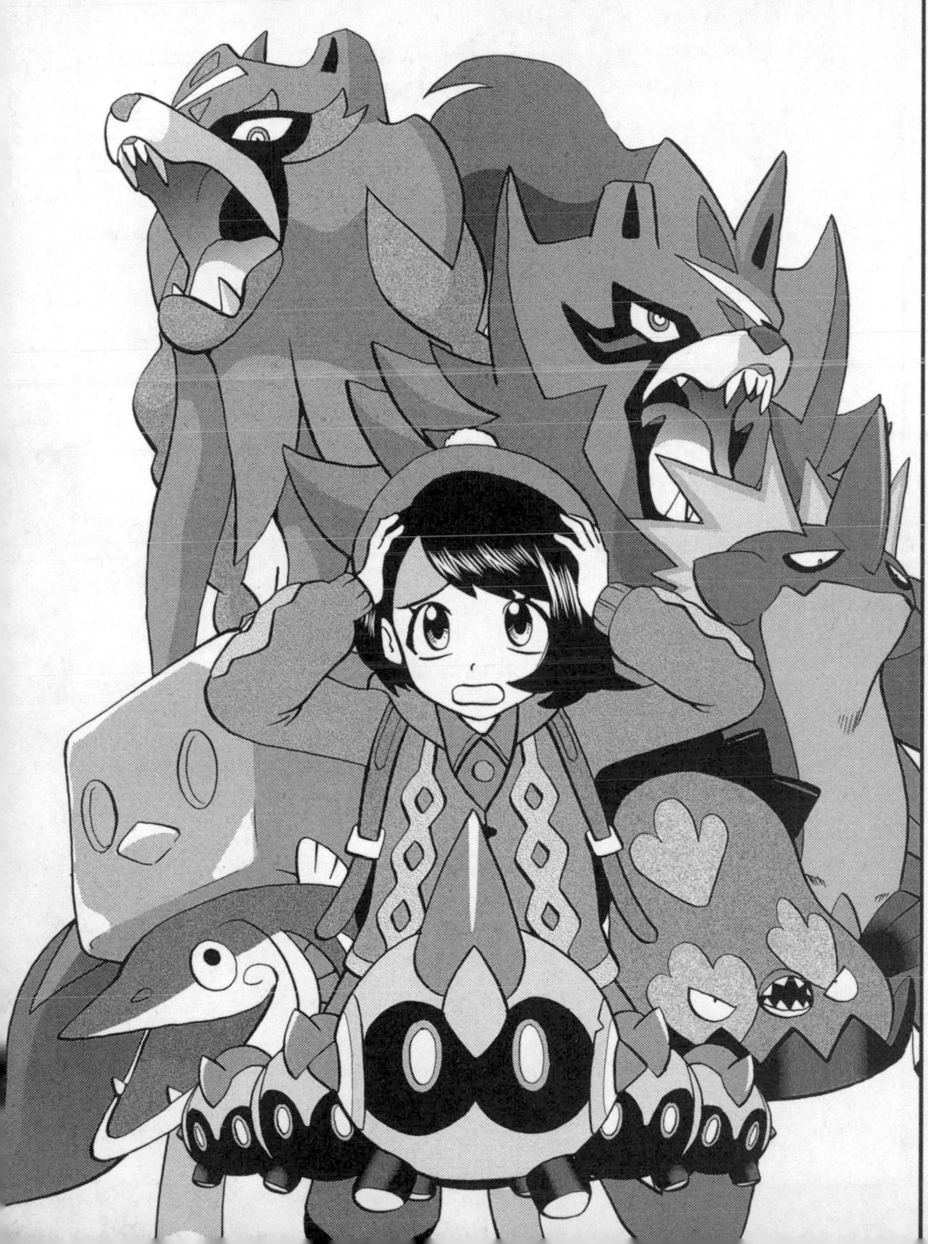

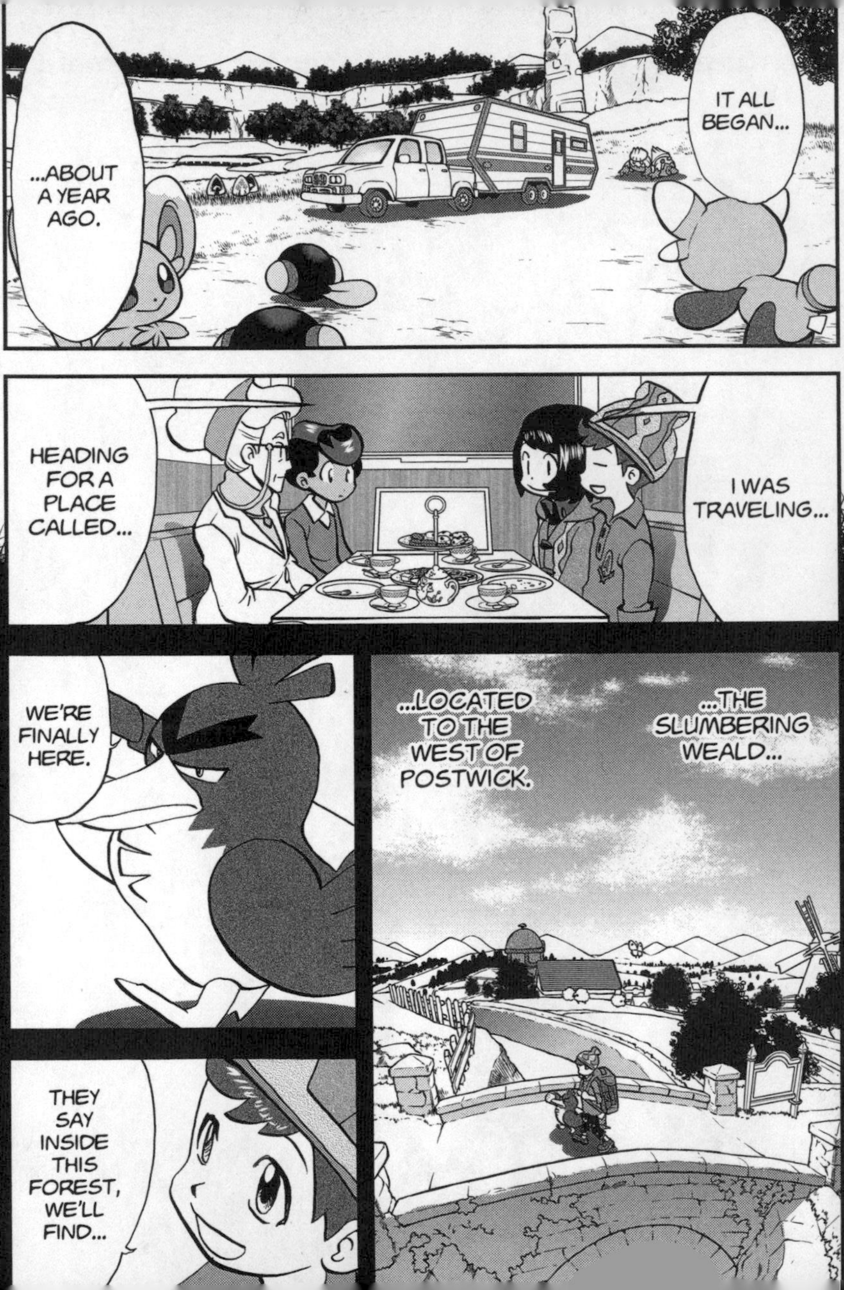
IT ALL BEGAN...
...ABOUT A YEAR AGO.
I WAS TRAVELING...
HEADING FOR A PLACE CALLED...
...THE SLUMBERING WEALD...
...LOCATED TO THE WEST OF POSTWICK.
WE'RE FINALLY HERE.
THEY SAY INSIDE THIS FOREST, WE'LL FIND...

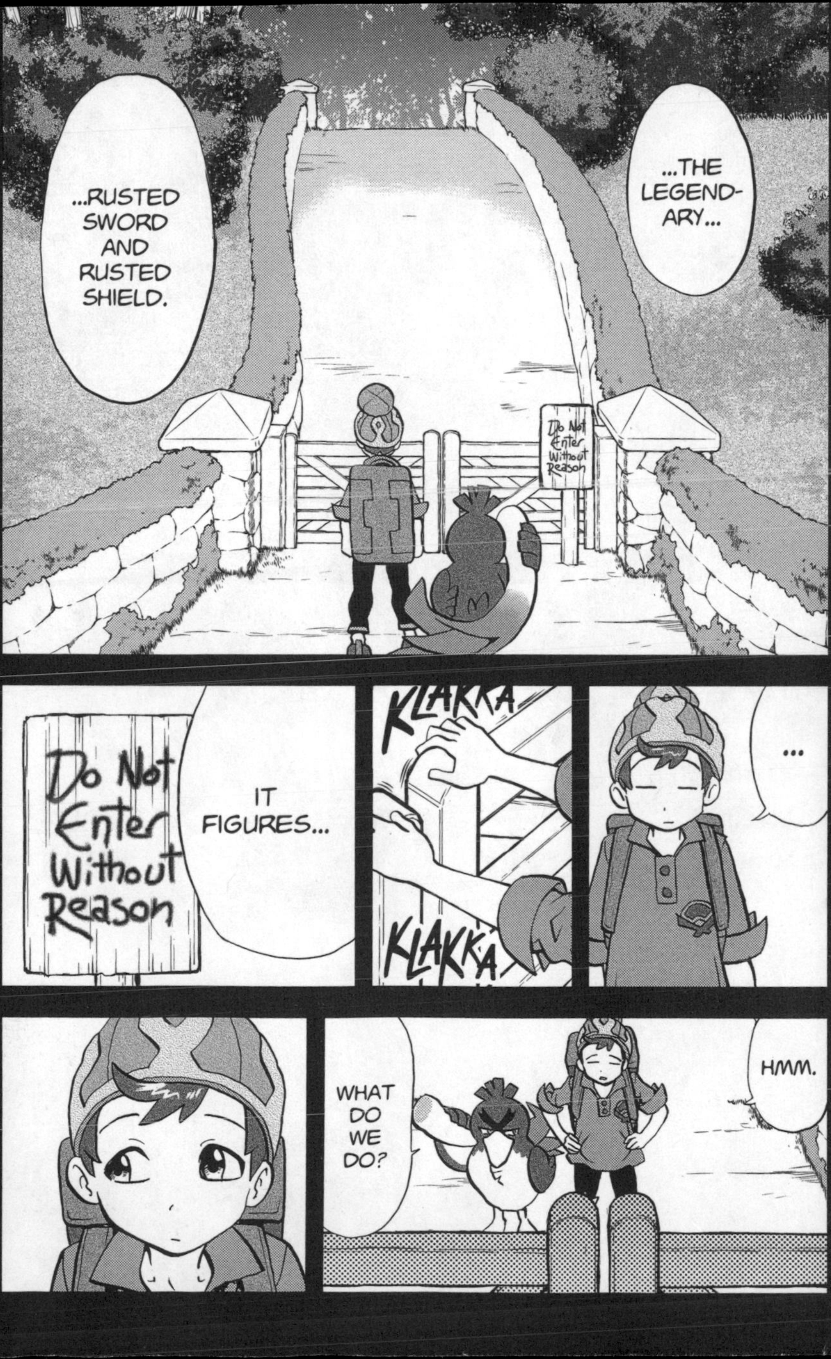
...THE LEGENDARY...
...RUSTED SWORD AND RUSTED SHIELD.
Do Not Enter Without Reason
...
KLAKKA
KLAKKA
IT FIGURES...
Do Not Enter Without Reason
HMM.
WHAT DO WE DO?

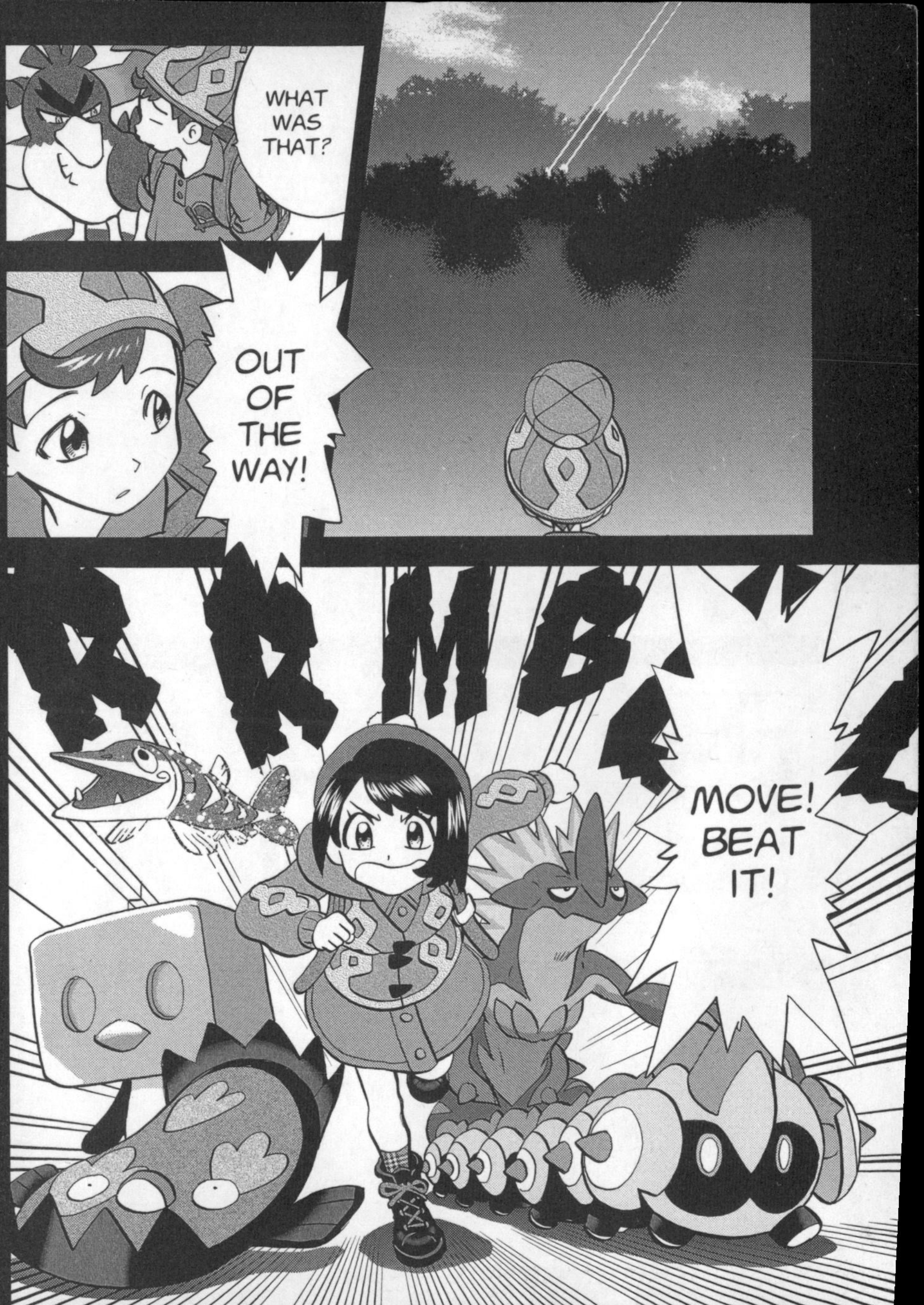
WHAT WAS THAT?
OUT OF THE WAY!
RRMB
MOVE! BEAT IT!

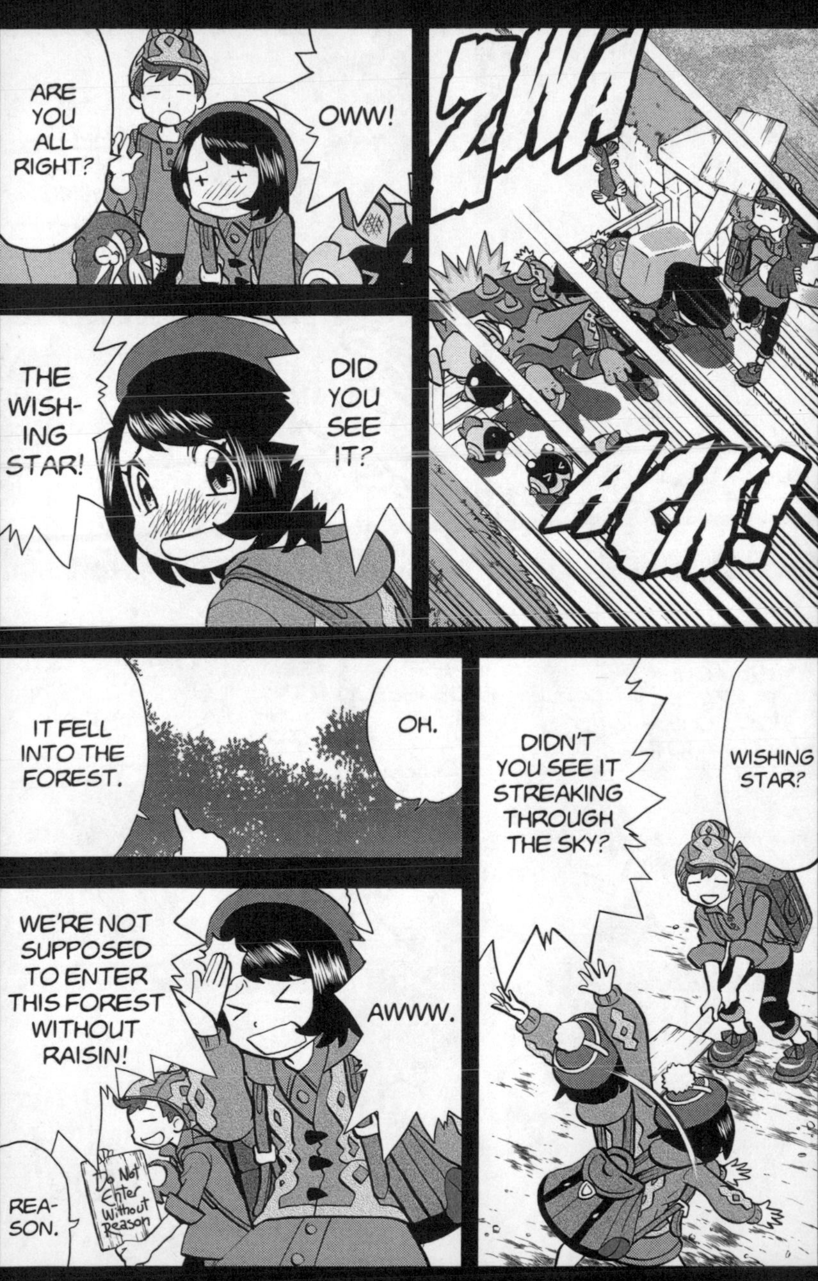
ZWA
ACK!
OWW!
ARE YOU ALL RIGHT?
DID YOU SEE IT?
THE WISH-ING STAR!
WISHING STAR?
DIDN'T YOU SEE IT STREAKING THROUGH THE SKY?
OH.
IT FELL INTO THE FOREST.
AWWW.
WE'RE NOT SUPPOSED TO ENTER THIS FOREST WITHOUT RAISIN!
Do Not Enter Without Reason
REA-SON.

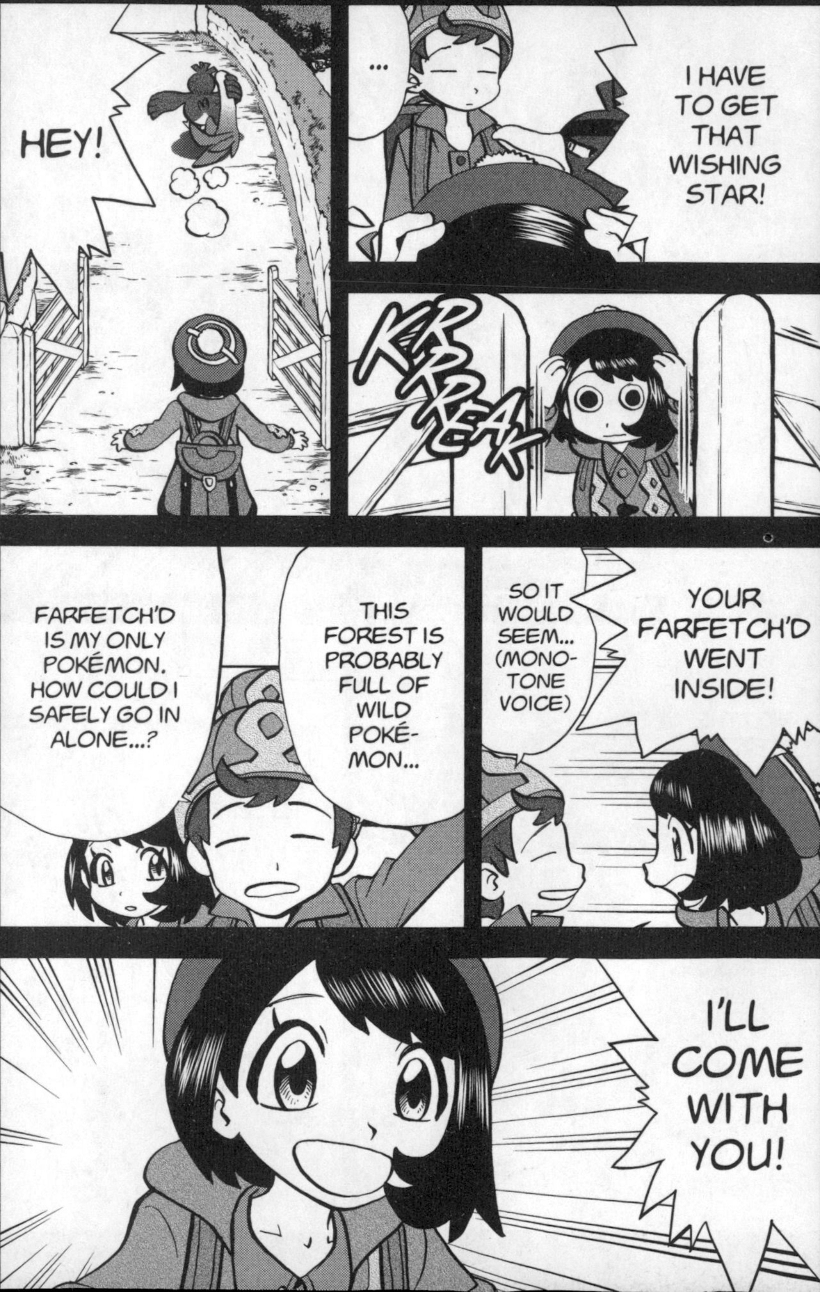
I HAVE TO GET THAT WISHING STAR!
...
KRREAK
HEY!
YOUR FARFETCH'D WENT INSIDE!
SO IT WOULD SEEM... (MONOTONE VOICE)
THIS FOREST IS PROBABLY FULL OF WILD POKÉMON...
FARFETCH'D IS MY ONLY POKÉMON. HOW COULD I SAFELY GO IN ALONE...?
I'LL COME WITH YOU!

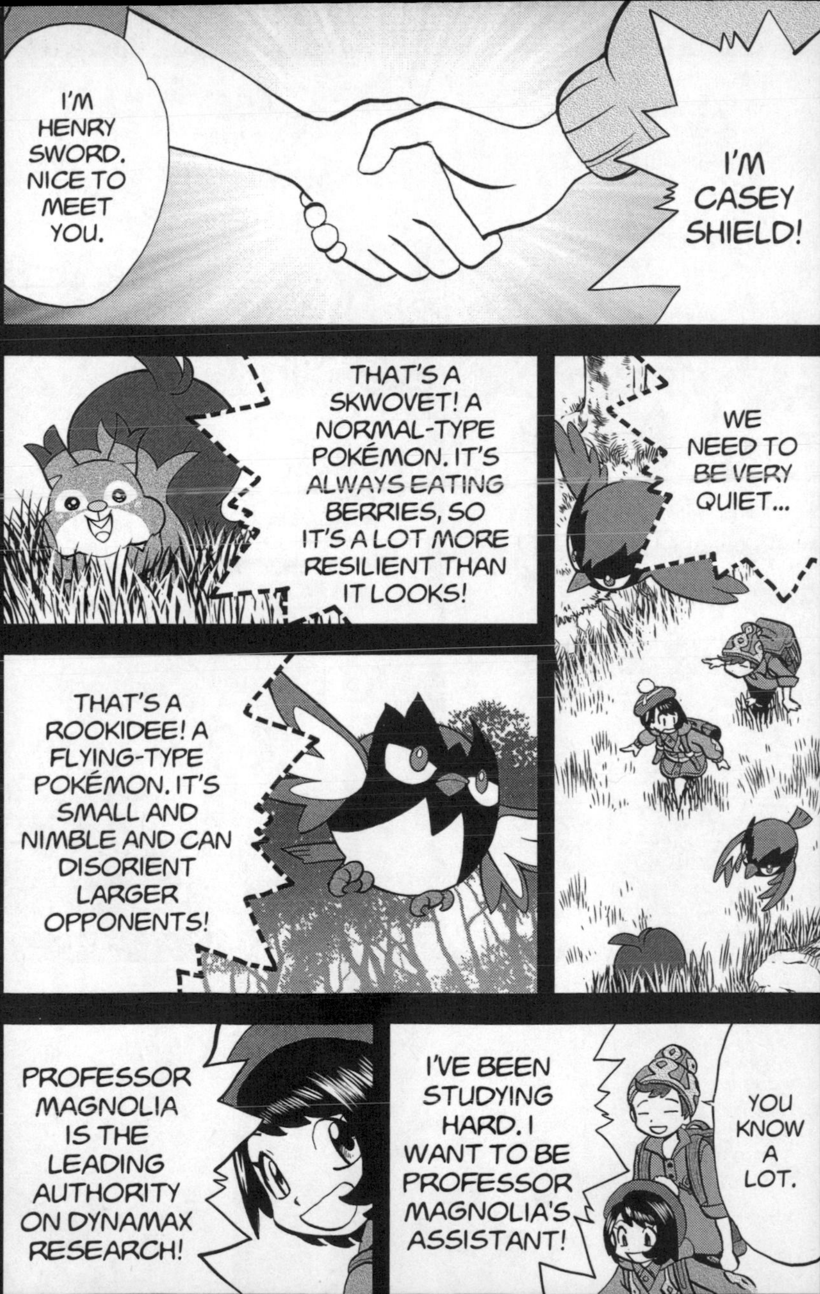
I'M CASEY SHIELD!
I'M HENRY SWORD. NICE TO MEET YOU.
WE NEED TO BE VERY QUIET...
THAT'S A SKWOVET! A NORMAL-TYPE POKÉMON. IT'S ALWAYS EATING BERRIES, SO IT'S A LOT MORE RESILIENT THAN IT LOOKS!
THAT'S A ROOKIDEE! A FLYING-TYPE POKÉMON. IT'S SMALL AND NIMBLE AND CAN DISORIENT LARGER OPPONENTS!
YOU KNOW A LOT.
I'VE BEEN STUDYING HARD. I WANT TO BE PROFESSOR MAGNOLIA'S ASSISTANT!
PROFESSOR MAGNOLIA IS THE LEADING AUTHORITY ON DYNAMAX RESEARCH!

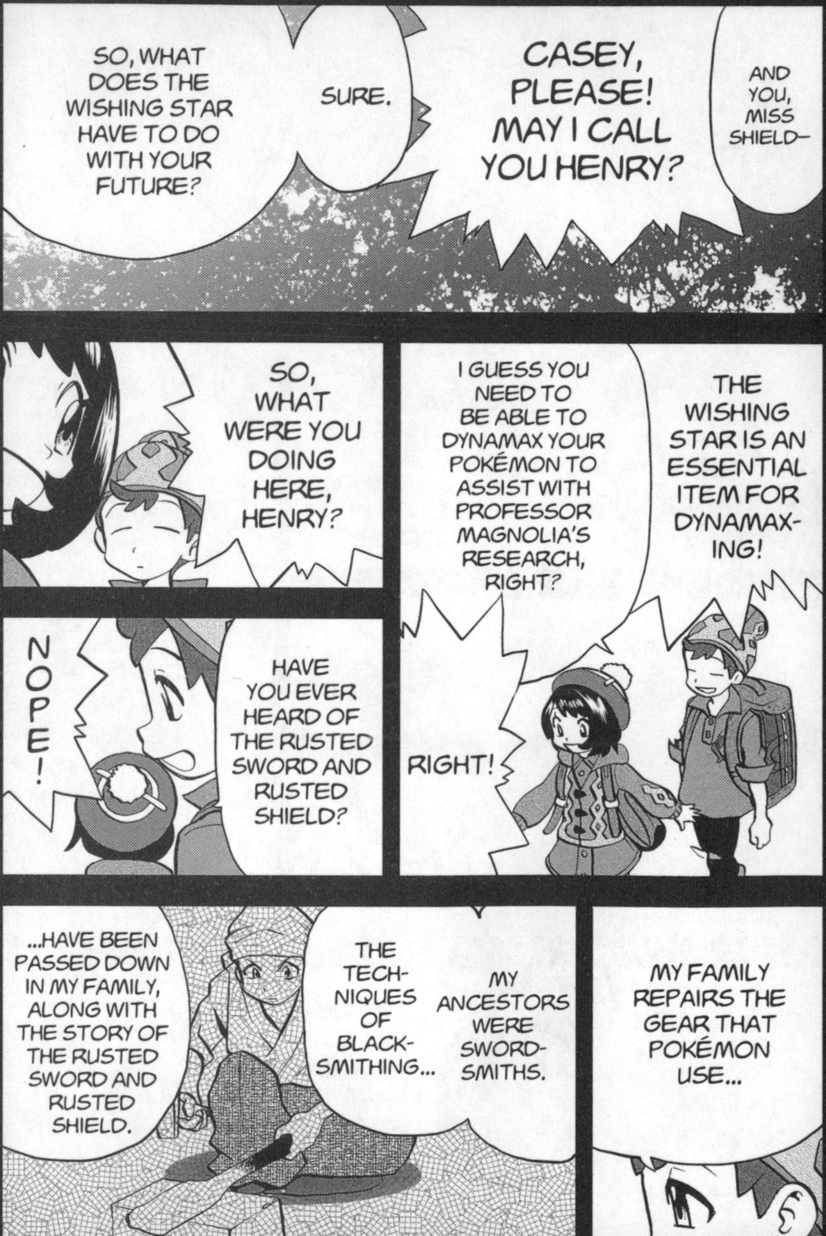
AND YOU, MISS SHIELD—
CASEY, PLEASE! MAY I CALL YOU HENRY?
SURE.
SO, WHAT DOES THE WISHING STAR HAVE TO DO WITH YOUR FUTURE?
THE WISHING STAR IS AN ESSENTIAL ITEM FOR DYNAMAX-ING!
I GUESS YOU NEED TO BE ABLE TO DYNAMAX YOUR POKÉMON TO ASSIST WITH PROFESSOR MAGNOLIA'S RESEARCH, RIGHT?
RIGHT!
SO, WHAT WERE YOU DOING HERE, HENRY?
HAVE YOU EVER HEARD OF THE RUSTED SWORD AND RUSTED SHIELD?
NOPE!
MY FAMILY REPAIRS THE GEAR THAT POKÉMON USE...
MY ANCESTORS WERE SWORD-SMITHS.
THE TECH-NIQUES OF BLACK-SMITHING...
...HAVE BEEN PASSED DOWN IN MY FAMILY, ALONG WITH THE STORY OF THE RUSTED SWORD AND RUSTED SHIELD.

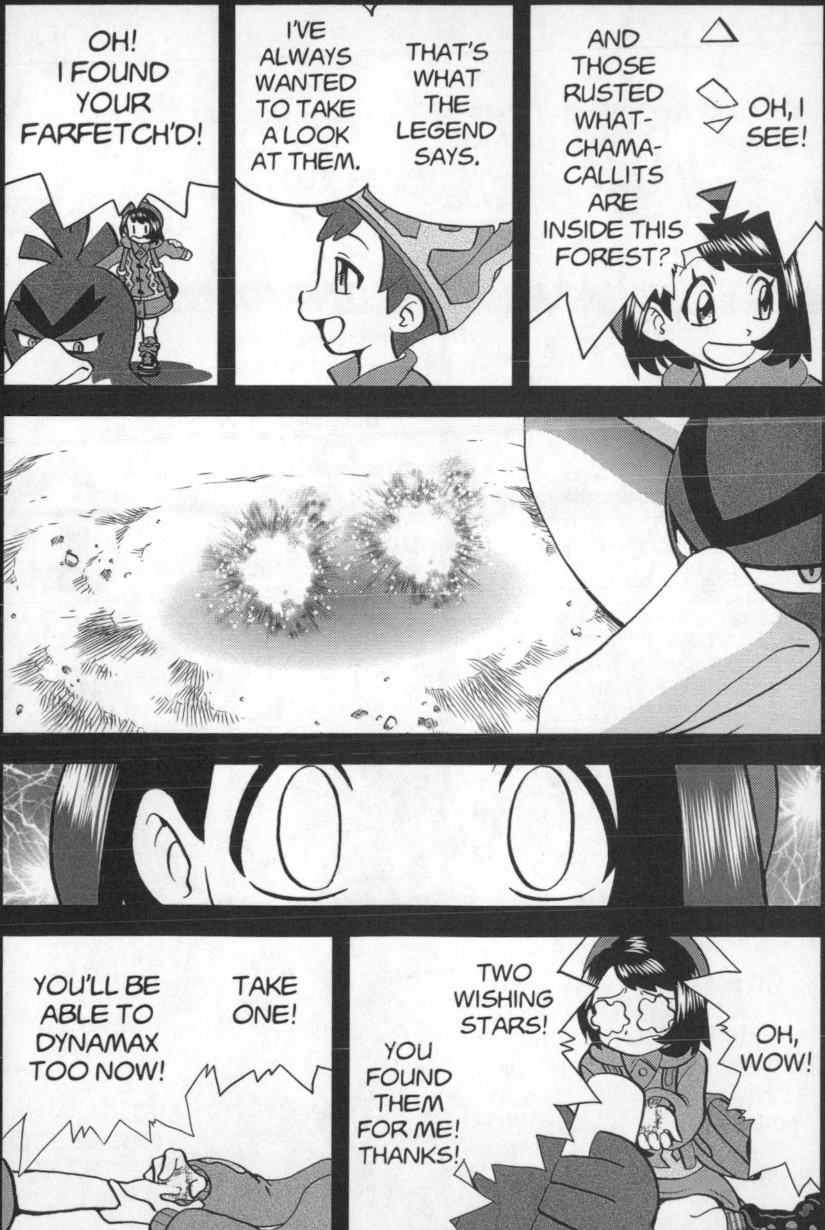
OH, I SEE!
AND THOSE RUSTED WHAT-CHAMA-CALLITS ARE INSIDE THIS FOREST?
THAT'S WHAT THE LEGEND SAYS.
I'VE ALWAYS WANTED TO TAKE A LOOK AT THEM.
OH! I FOUND YOUR FARFETCH'D!
OH, WOW!
TWO WISHING STARS!
YOU FOUND THEM FOR ME! THANKS!
TAKE ONE!
YOU'LL BE ABLE TO DYNAMAX TOO NOW!

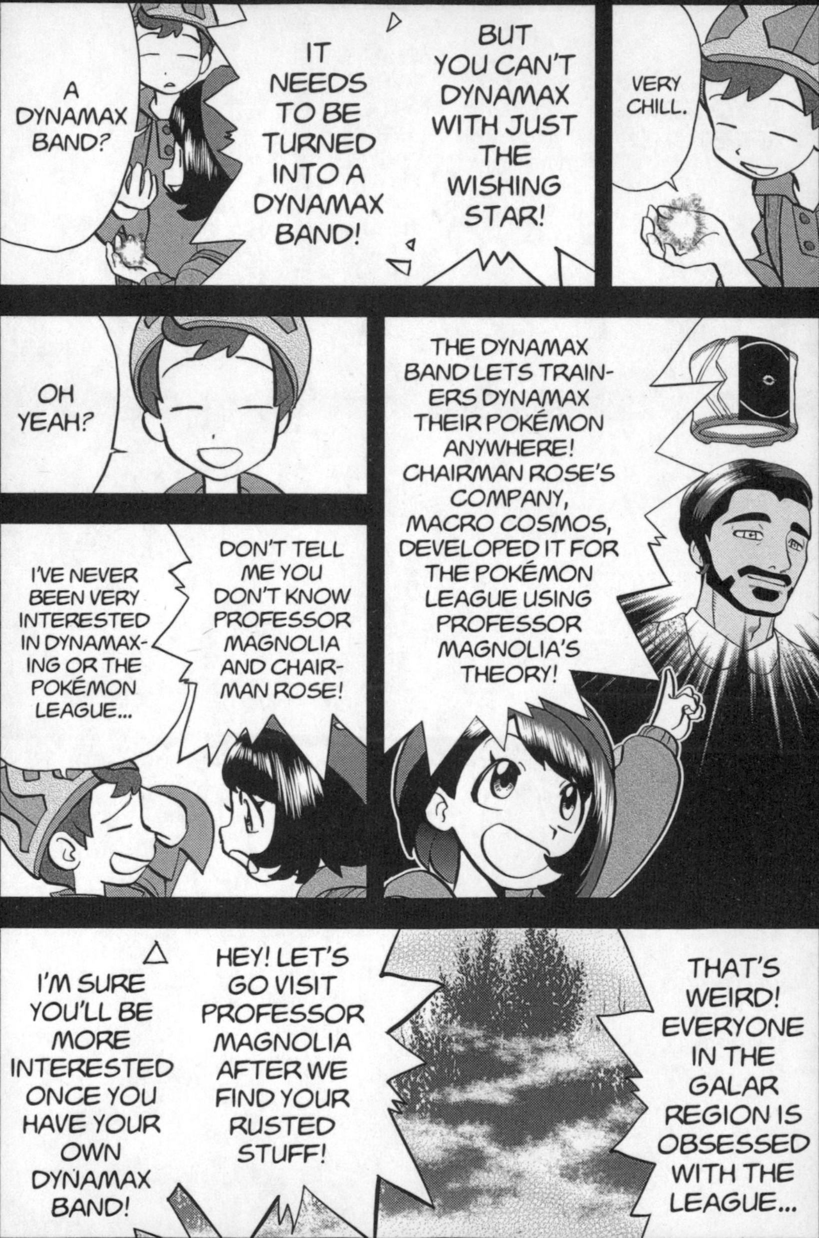
VERY CHILL.
BUT YOU CAN'T DYNAMAX WITH JUST THE WISHING STAR!
IT NEEDS TO BE TURNED INTO A DYNAMAX BAND!
A DYNAMAX BAND?
THE DYNAMAX BAND LETS TRAIN-ERS DYNAMAX THEIR POKÉMON ANYWHERE! CHAIRMAN ROSE'S COMPANY, MACRO COSMOS, DEVELOPED IT FOR THE POKÉMON LEAGUE USING PROFESSOR MAGNOLIA'S THEORY!
OH YEAH?
DON'T TELL ME YOU DON'T KNOW PROFESSOR MAGNOLIA AND CHAIR-MAN ROSE!
I'VE NEVER BEEN VERY INTERESTED IN DYNAMAX-ING OR THE POKÉMON LEAGUE...
THAT'S WEIRD! EVERYONE IN THE GALAR REGION IS OBSESSED WITH THE LEAGUE...
HEY! LET'S GO VISIT PROFESSOR MAGNOLIA AFTER WE FIND YOUR RUSTED STUFF!
I'M SURE YOU'LL BE MORE INTERESTED ONCE YOU HAVE YOUR OWN DYNAMAX BAND!

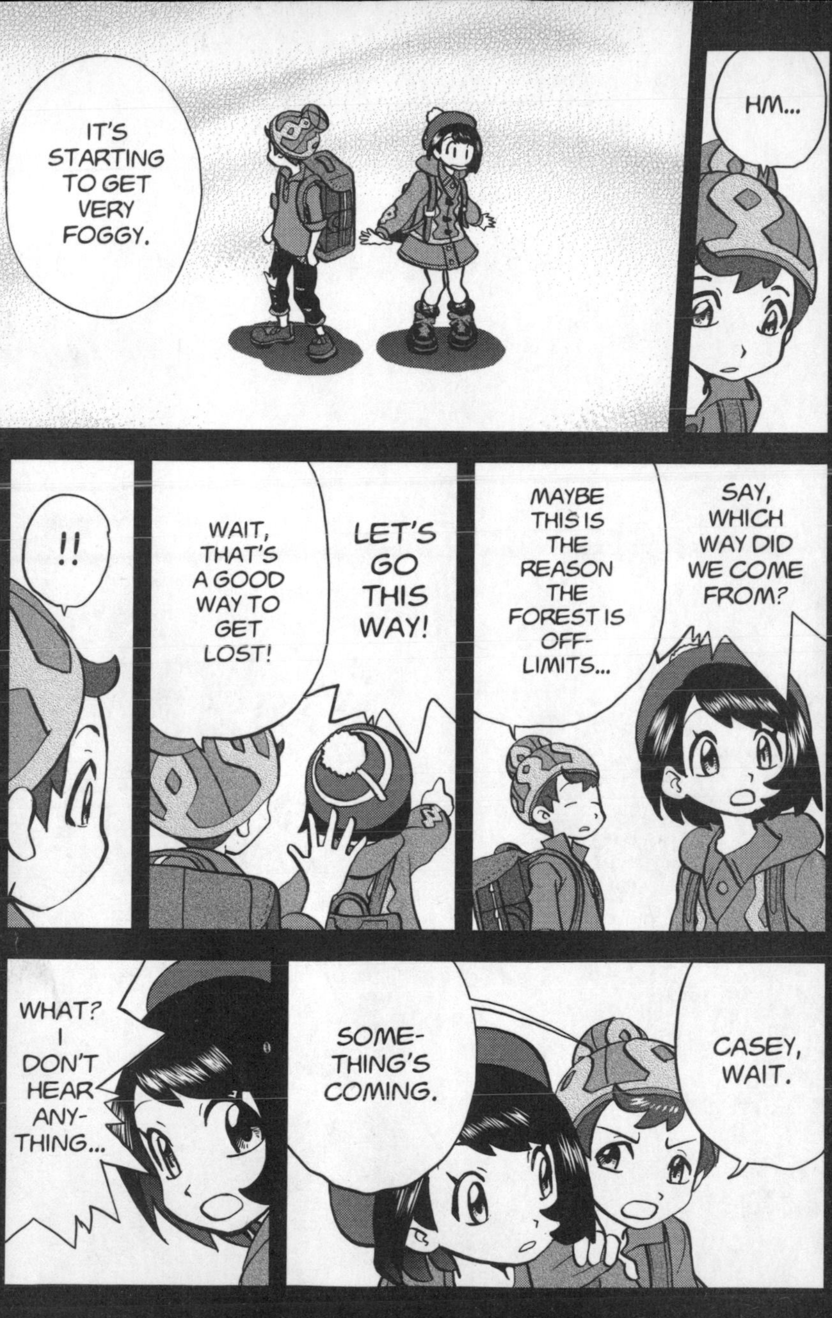
HM...
IT'S STARTING TO GET VERY FOGGY.
SAY, WHICH WAY DID WE COME FROM?
MAYBE THIS IS THE REASON THE FOREST IS OFF-LIMITS...
LET'S GO THIS WAY!
WAIT, THAT'S A GOOD WAY TO GET LOST!
!!
CASEY, WAIT.
SOME-THING'S COMING.
WHAT? I DON'T HEAR ANY-THING...

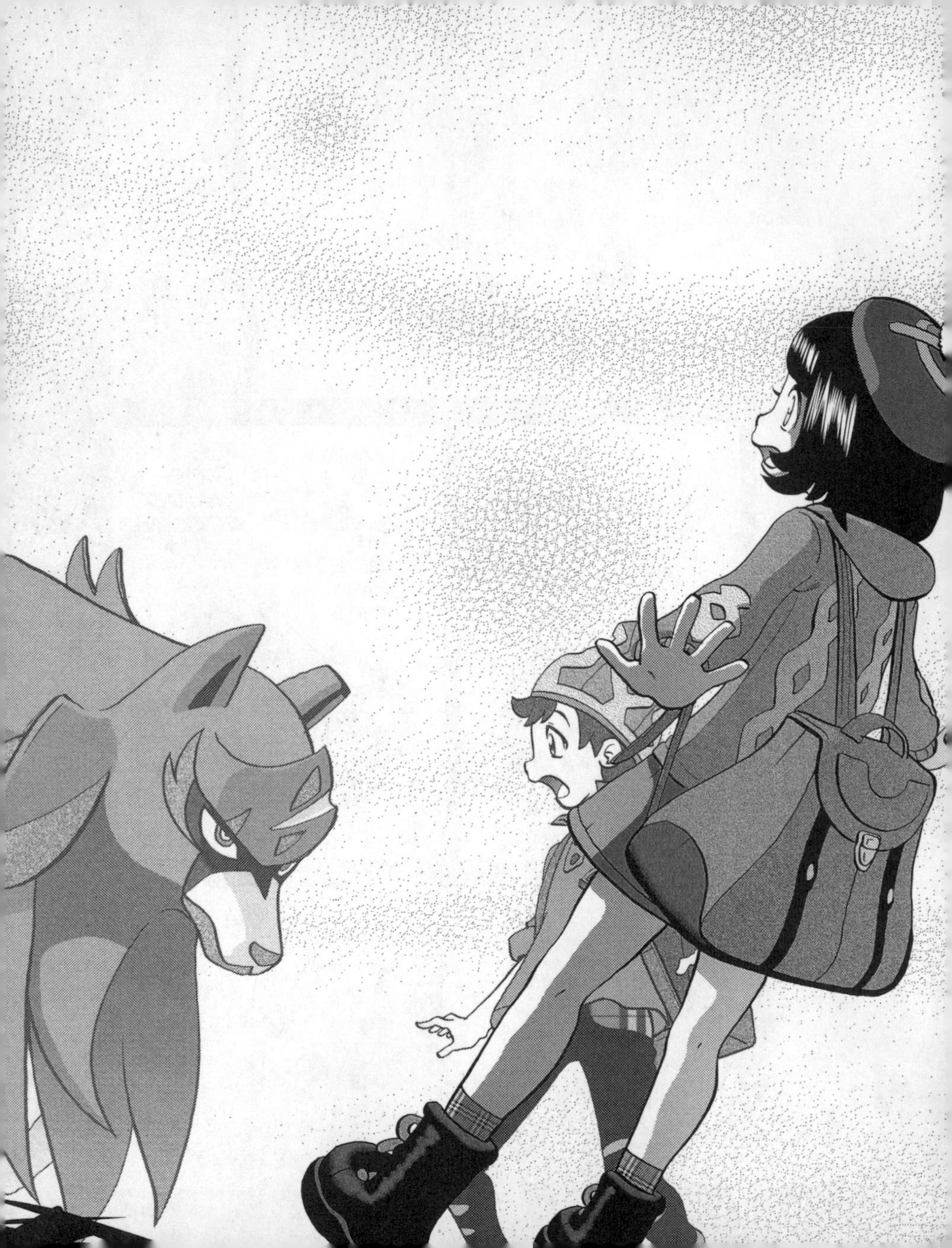

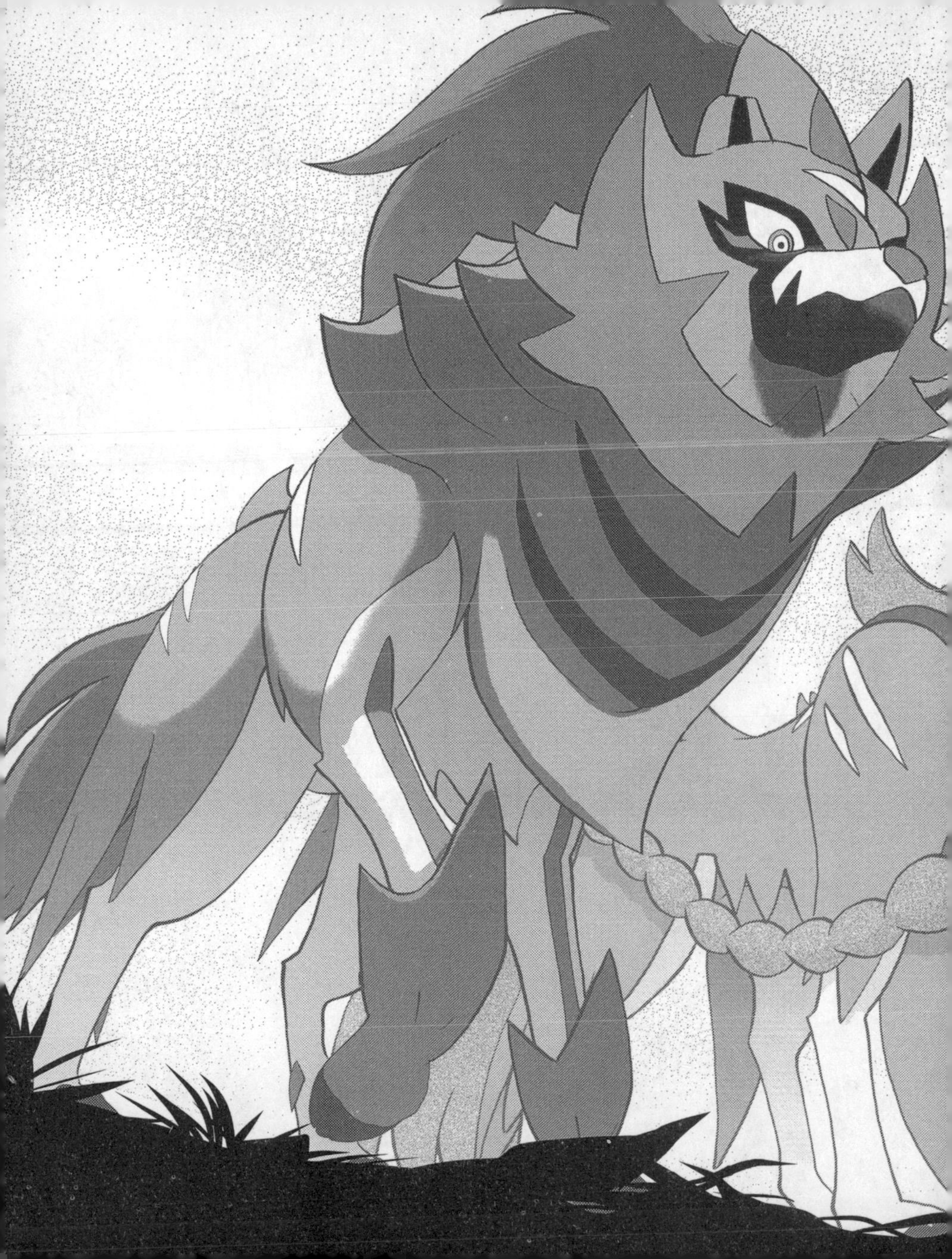

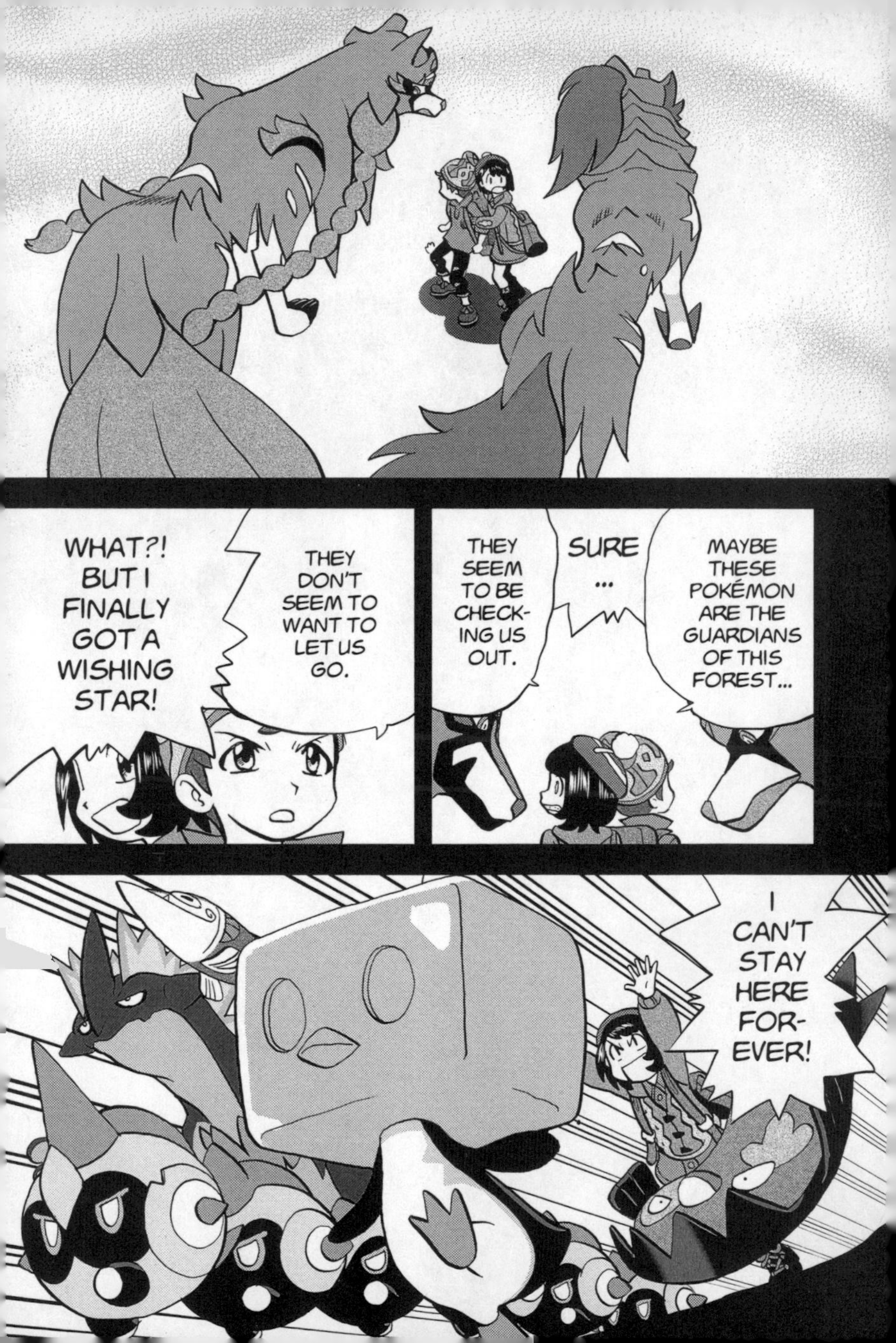
MAYBE THESE POKÉMON ARE THE GUARDIANS OF THIS FOREST...
SURE ...
THEY SEEM TO BE CHECK-ING US OUT.
THEY DON'T SEEM TO WANT TO LET US GO.
WHAT?! BUT I FINALLY GOT A WISHING STAR!
I CAN'T STAY HERE FOR-EVER!

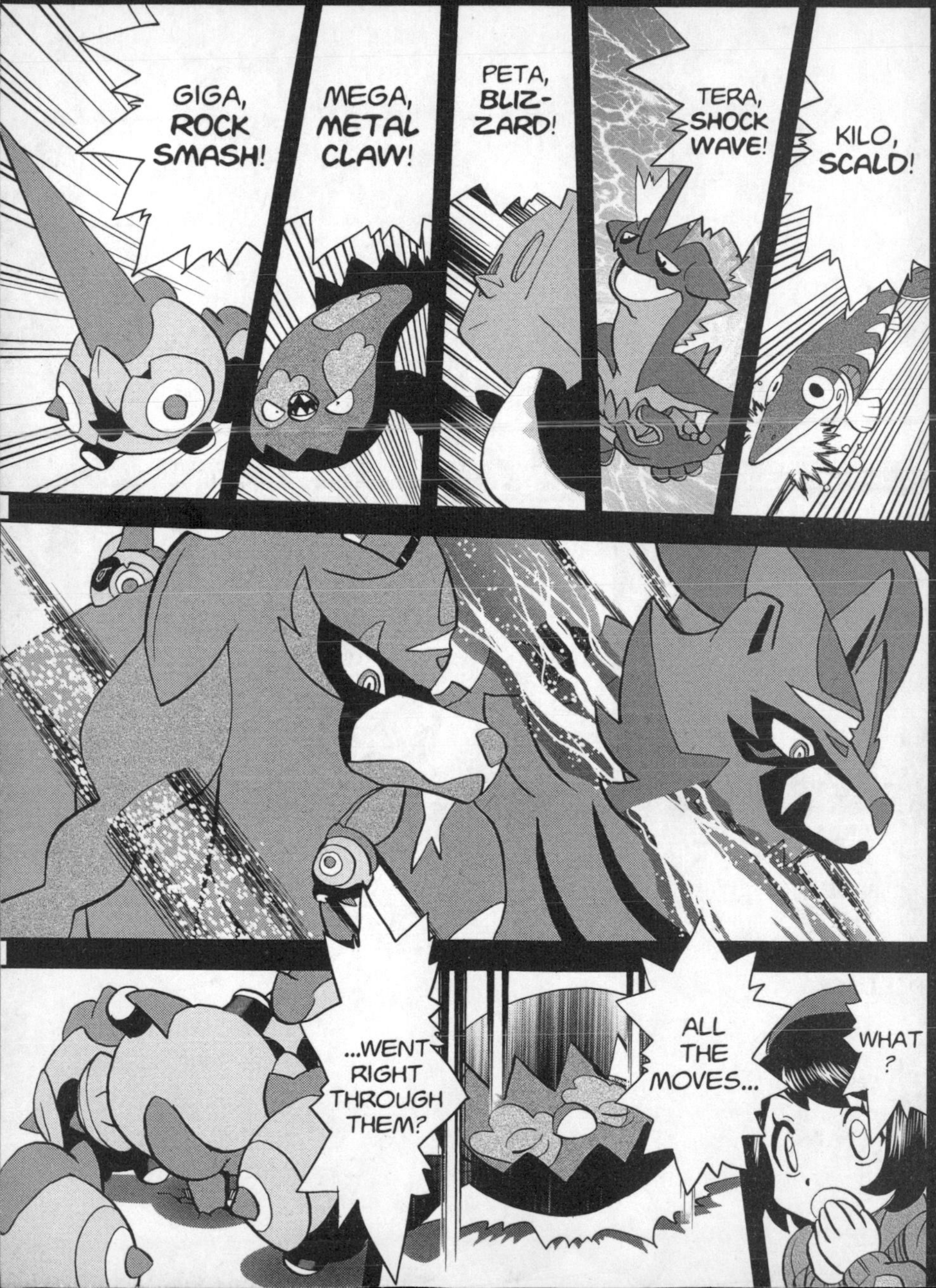
KILO, SCALD!
TERA, SHOCK WAVE!
PETA, BLIZ-ZARD!
MEGA, METAL CLAW!
GIGA, ROCK SMASH!
WHAT?
ALL THE MOVES...
...WENT RIGHT THROUGH THEM?

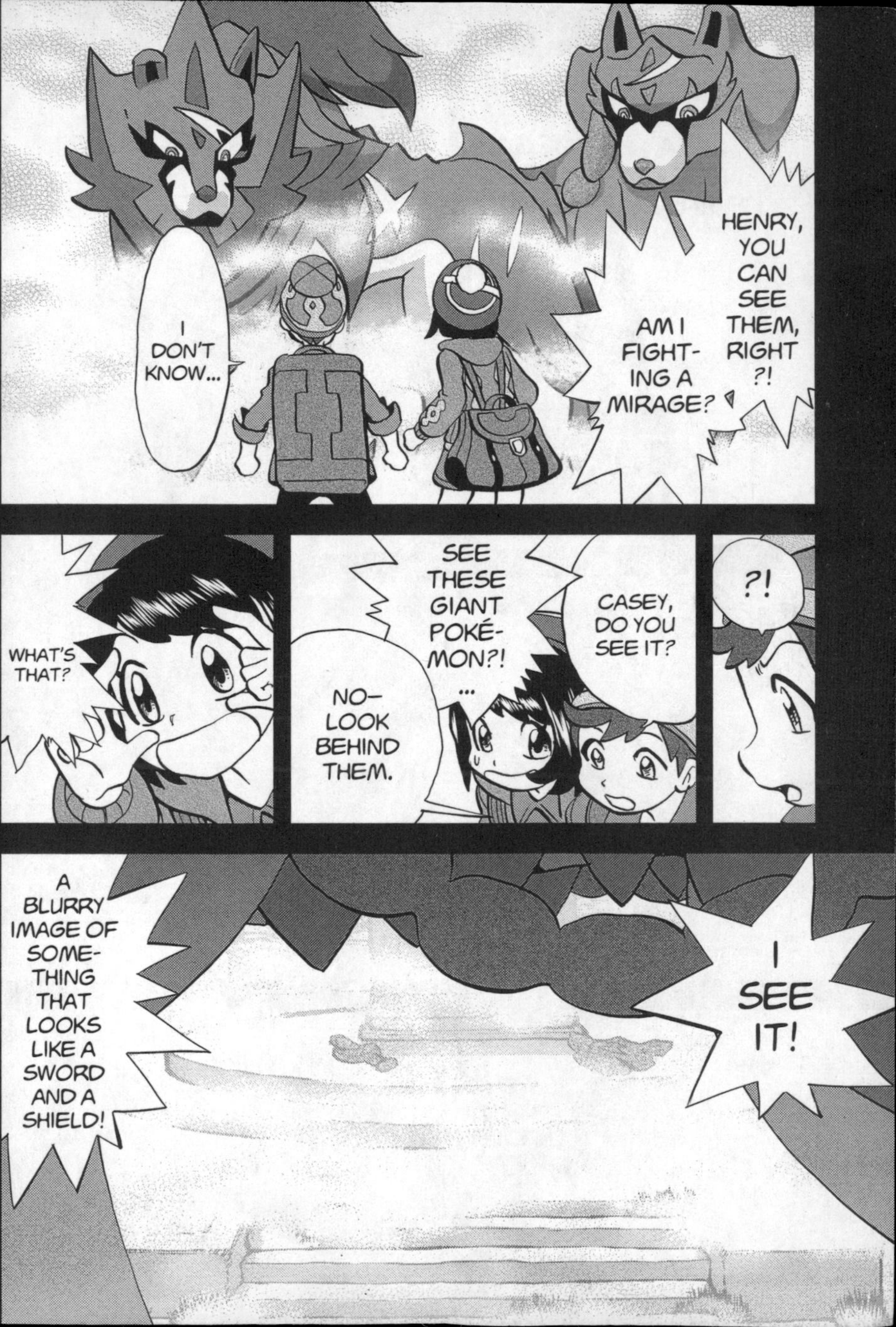
HENRY, YOU CAN SEE THEM, RIGHT?!
AM I FIGHTING A MIRAGE?
I DON'T KNOW...
?!
CASEY, DO YOU SEE IT?
SEE THESE GIANT POKÉMON?!
...
NO— LOOK BEHIND THEM.
WHAT'S THAT?
I SEE IT!
A BLURRY IMAGE OF SOMETHING THAT LOOKS LIKE A SWORD AND A SHIELD!

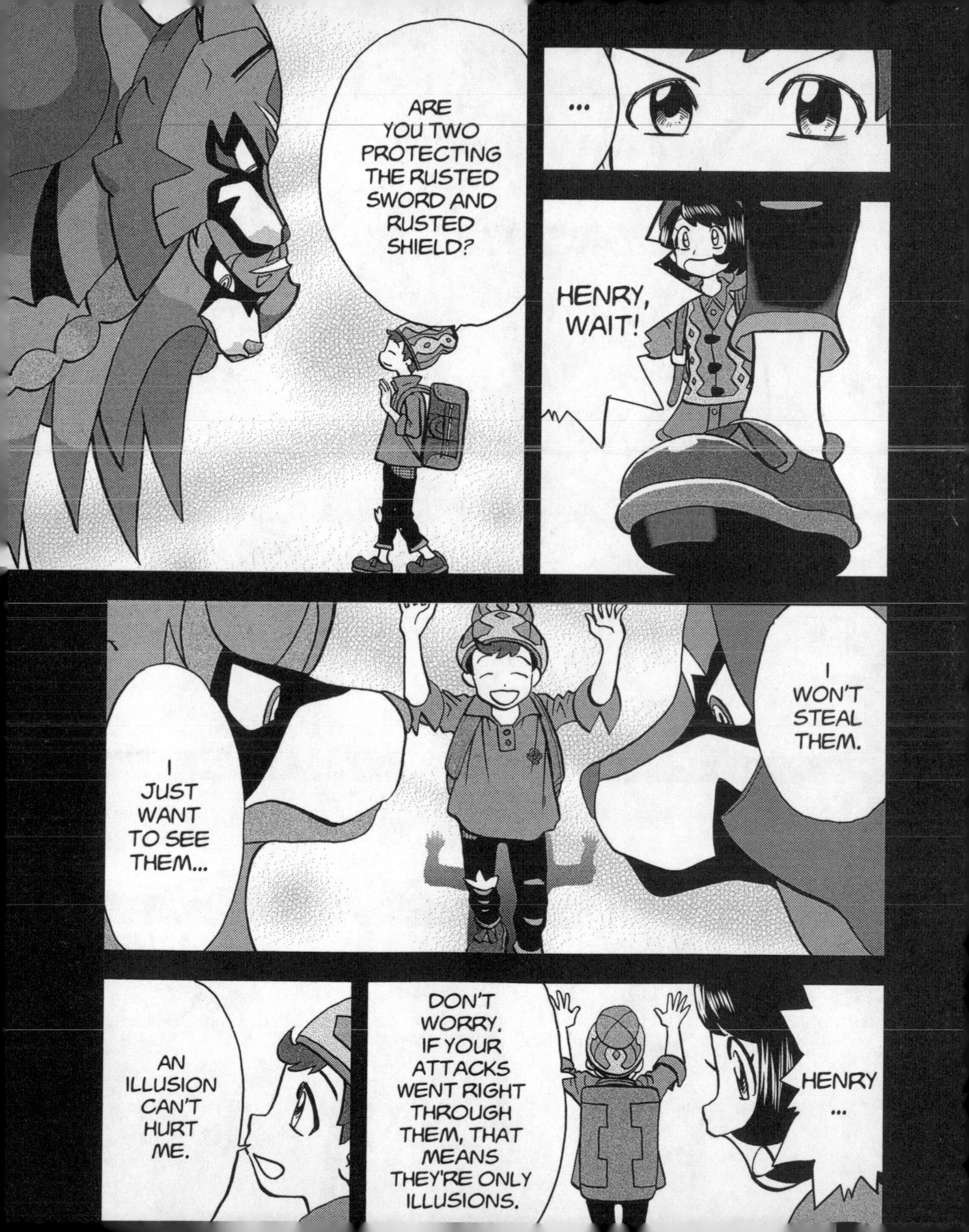
...
HENRY, WAIT!
ARE YOU TWO PROTECTING THE RUSTED SWORD AND RUSTED SHIELD?
I WON'T STEAL THEM.
I JUST WANT TO SEE THEM...
HENRY...
DON'T WORRY. IF YOUR ATTACKS WENT RIGHT THROUGH THEM, THAT MEANS THEY'RE ONLY ILLUSIONS.
AN ILLUSION CAN'T HURT ME.

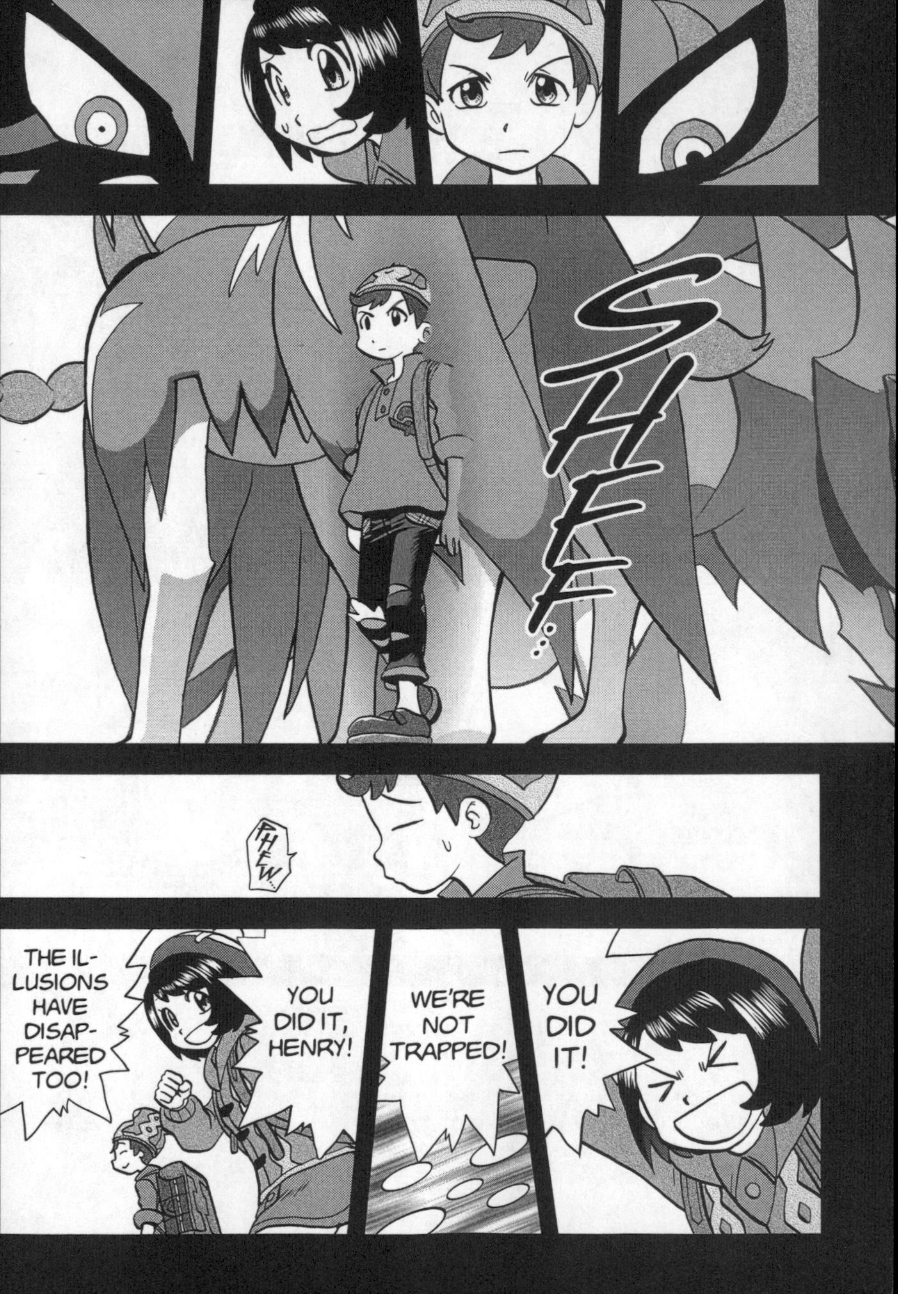
SHEEE...
PHEW...
YOU DID IT!
WE'RE NOT TRAPPED!
YOU DID IT, HENRY!
THE ILLUSIONS HAVE DISAPPEARED TOO!

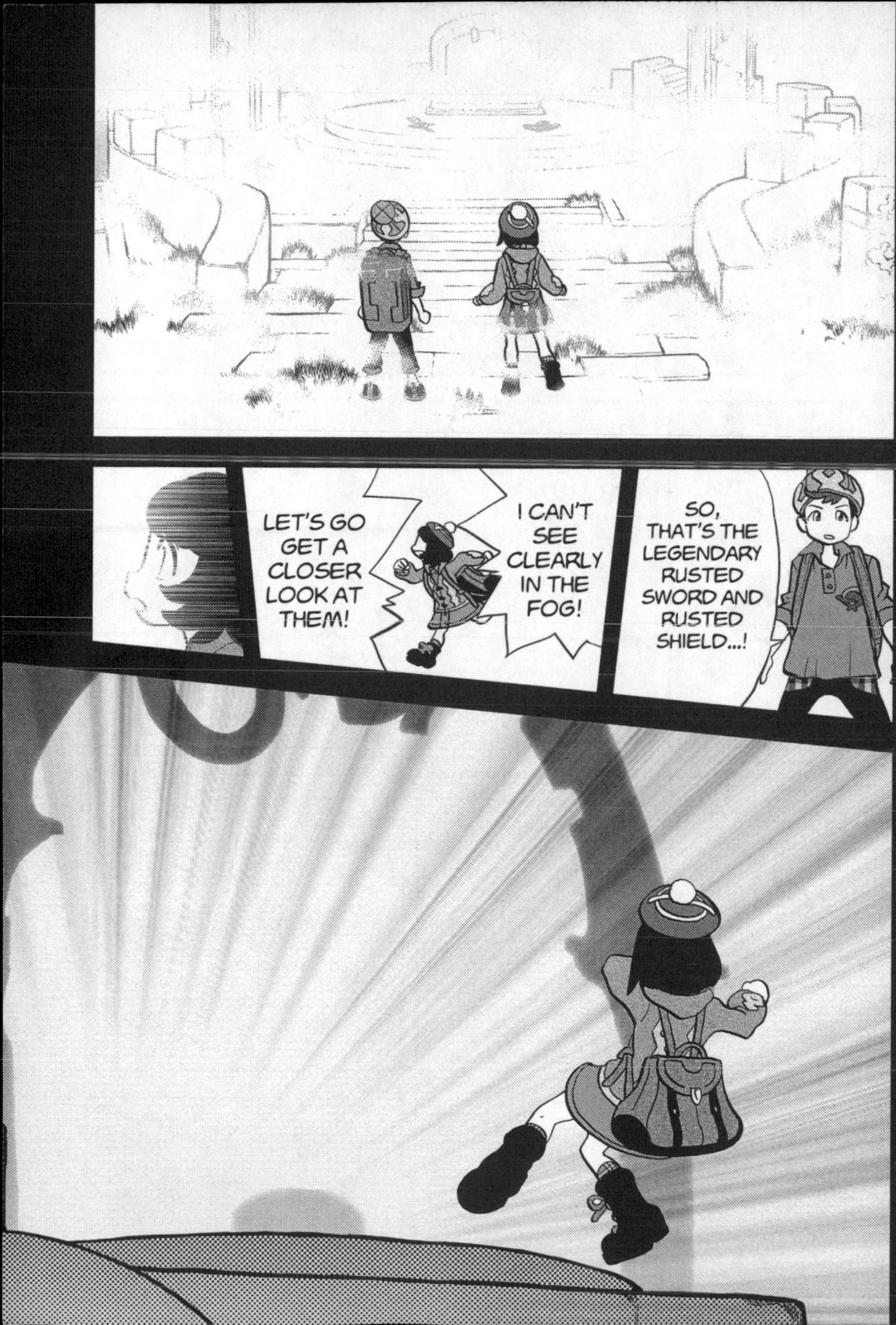
SO, THAT'S THE LEGENDARY RUSTED SWORD AND RUSTED SHIELD...!
I CAN'T SEE CLEARLY IN THE FOG!
LET'S GO GET A CLOSER LOOK AT THEM!

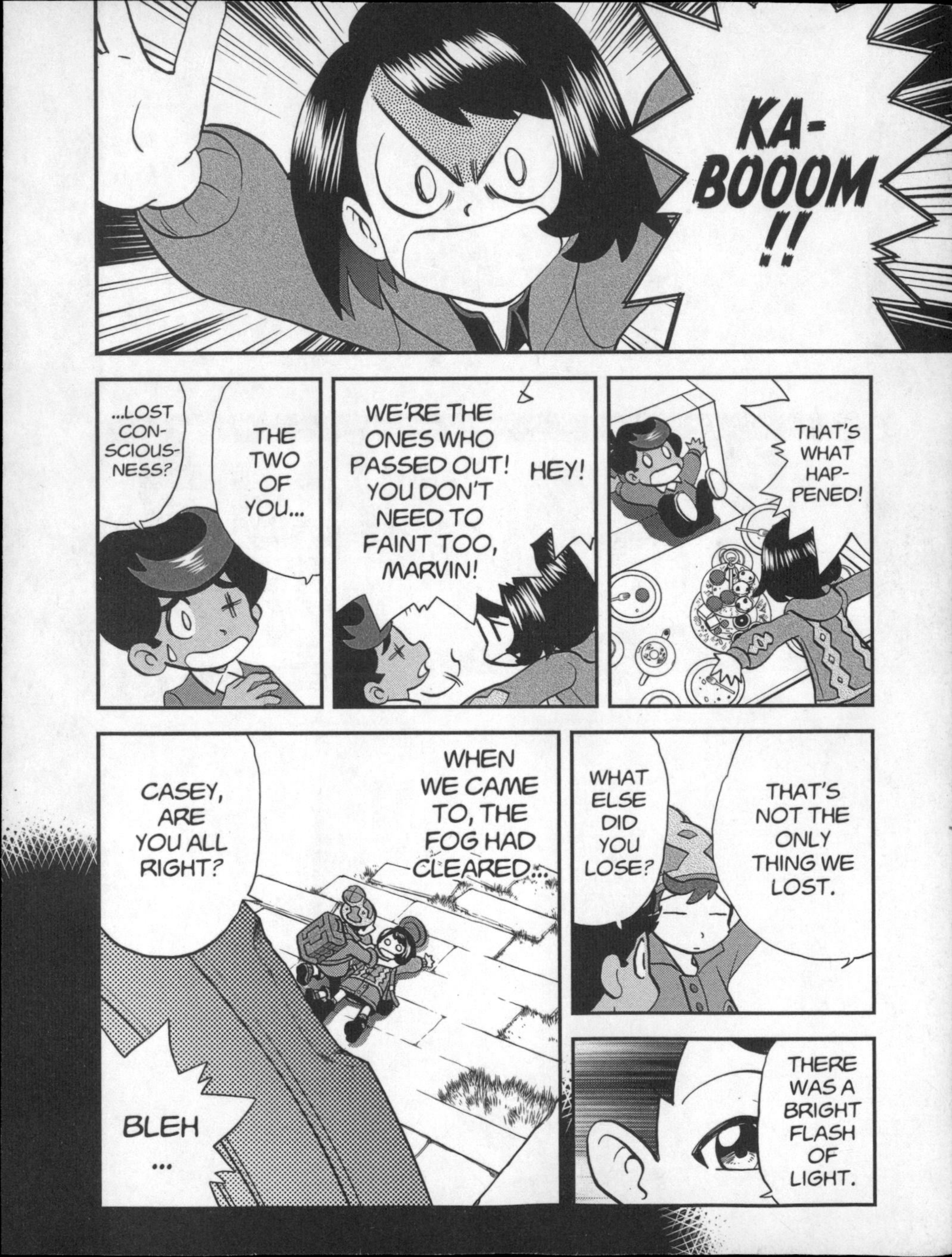
KA-BOOOM!!
THAT'S WHAT HAPPENED!
HEY!
WE'RE THE ONES WHO PASSED OUT! YOU DON'T NEED TO FAINT TOO, MARVIN!
THE TWO OF YOU...
...LOST CONSCIOUSNESS?
THAT'S NOT THE ONLY THING WE LOST.
WHAT ELSE DID YOU LOSE?
THERE WAS A BRIGHT FLASH OF LIGHT.
WHEN WE CAME TO, THE FOG HAD CLEARED...
CASEY, ARE YOU ALL RIGHT?
BLEH...

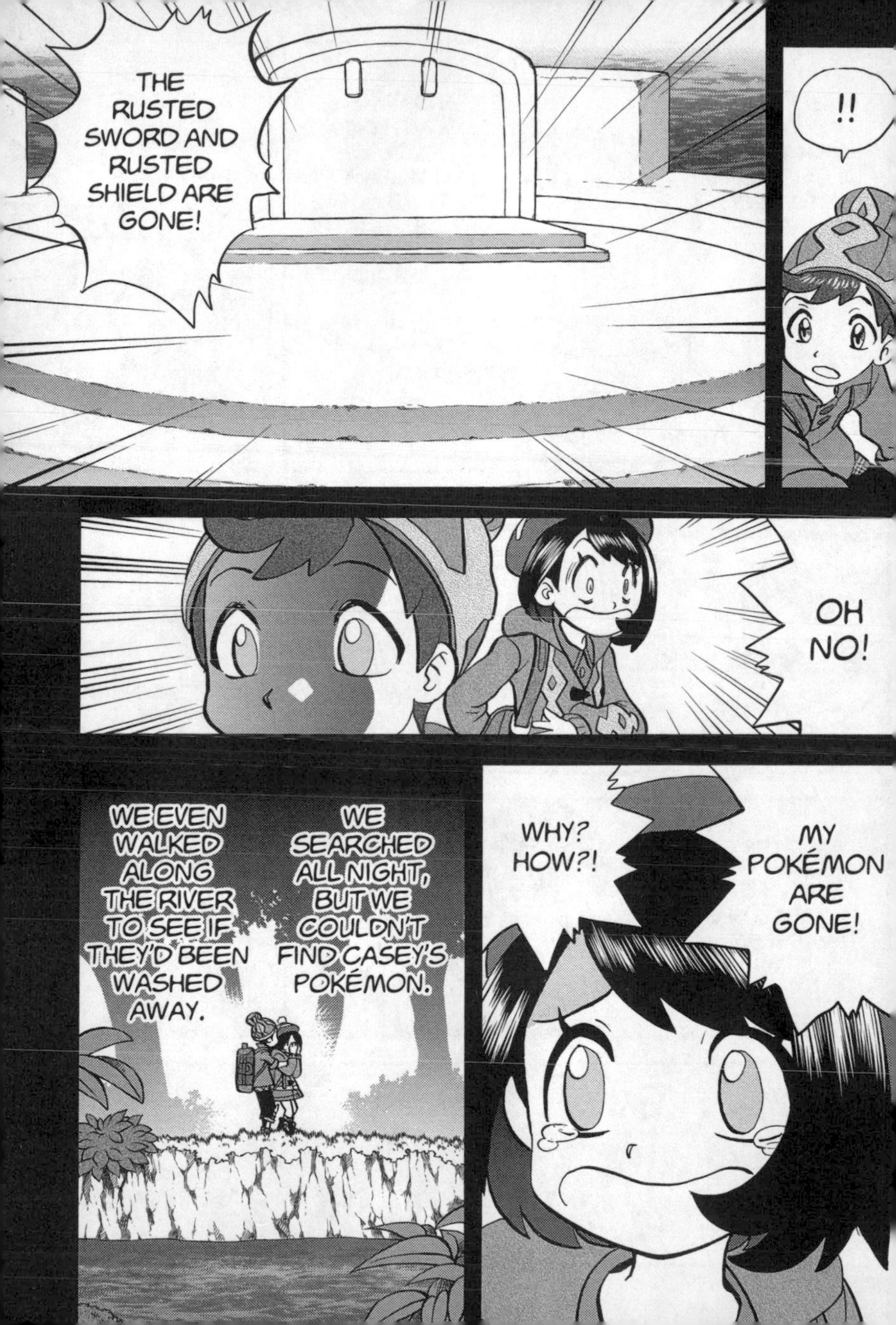
!!
THE RUSTED SWORD AND RUSTED SHIELD ARE GONE!
OH NO!
MY POKÉMON ARE GONE!
WHY? HOW?!
WE SEARCHED ALL NIGHT, BUT WE COULDN'T FIND CASEY'S POKÉMON.
WE EVEN WALKED ALONG THE RIVER TO SEE IF THEY'D BEEN WASHED AWAY.

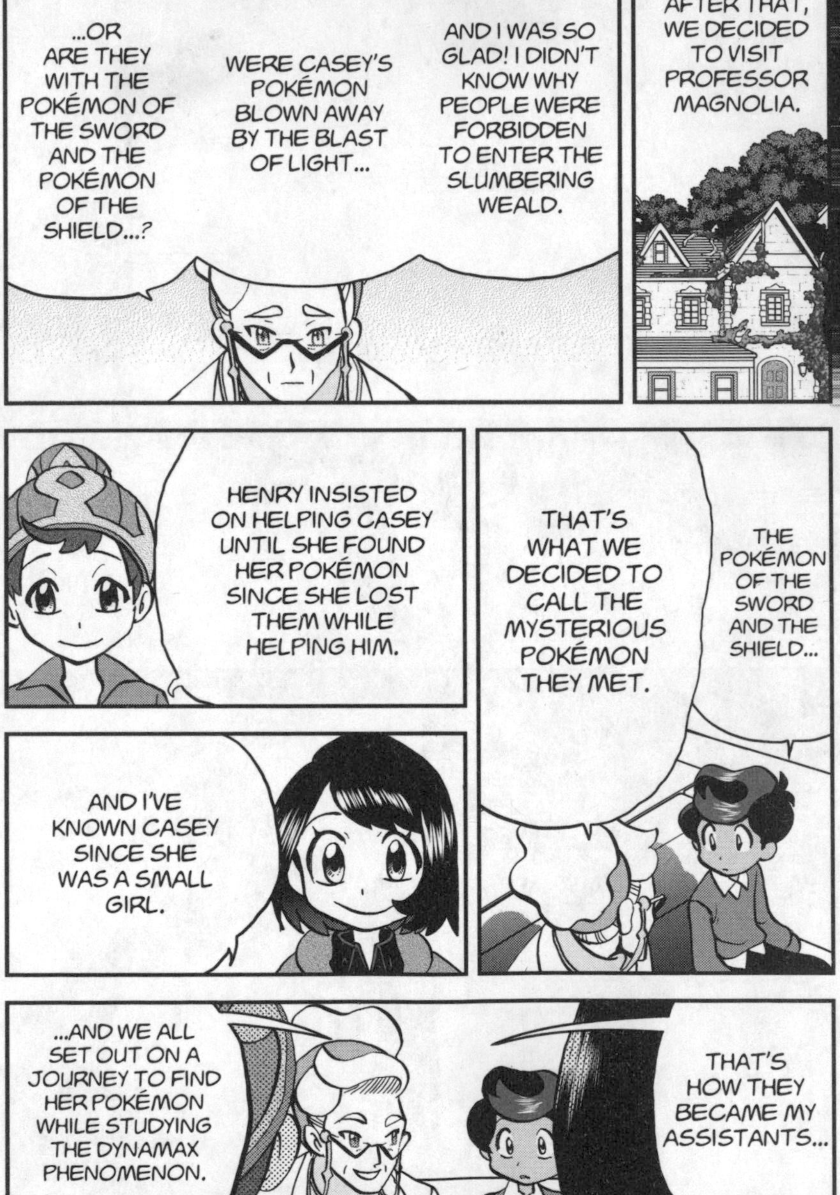
AFTER THAT, WE DECIDED TO VISIT PROFESSOR MAGNOLIA.
AND I WAS SO GLAD! I DIDN'T KNOW WHY PEOPLE WERE FORBIDDEN TO ENTER THE SLUMBERING WEALD.
WERE CASEY'S POKÉMON BLOWN AWAY BY THE BLAST OF LIGHT...
...OR ARE THEY WITH THE POKÉMON OF THE SWORD AND THE POKÉMON OF THE SHIELD...?
THE POKÉMON OF THE SWORD AND THE SHIELD...
THAT'S WHAT WE DECIDED TO CALL THE MYSTERIOUS POKÉMON THEY MET.
HENRY INSISTED ON HELPING CASEY UNTIL SHE FOUND HER POKÉMON SINCE SHE LOST THEM WHILE HELPING HIM.
AND I'VE KNOWN CASEY SINCE SHE WAS A SMALL GIRL.
THAT'S HOW THEY BECAME MY ASSISTANTS...
...AND WE ALL SET OUT ON A JOURNEY TO FIND HER POKÉMON WHILE STUDYING THE DYNAMAX PHENOMENON.

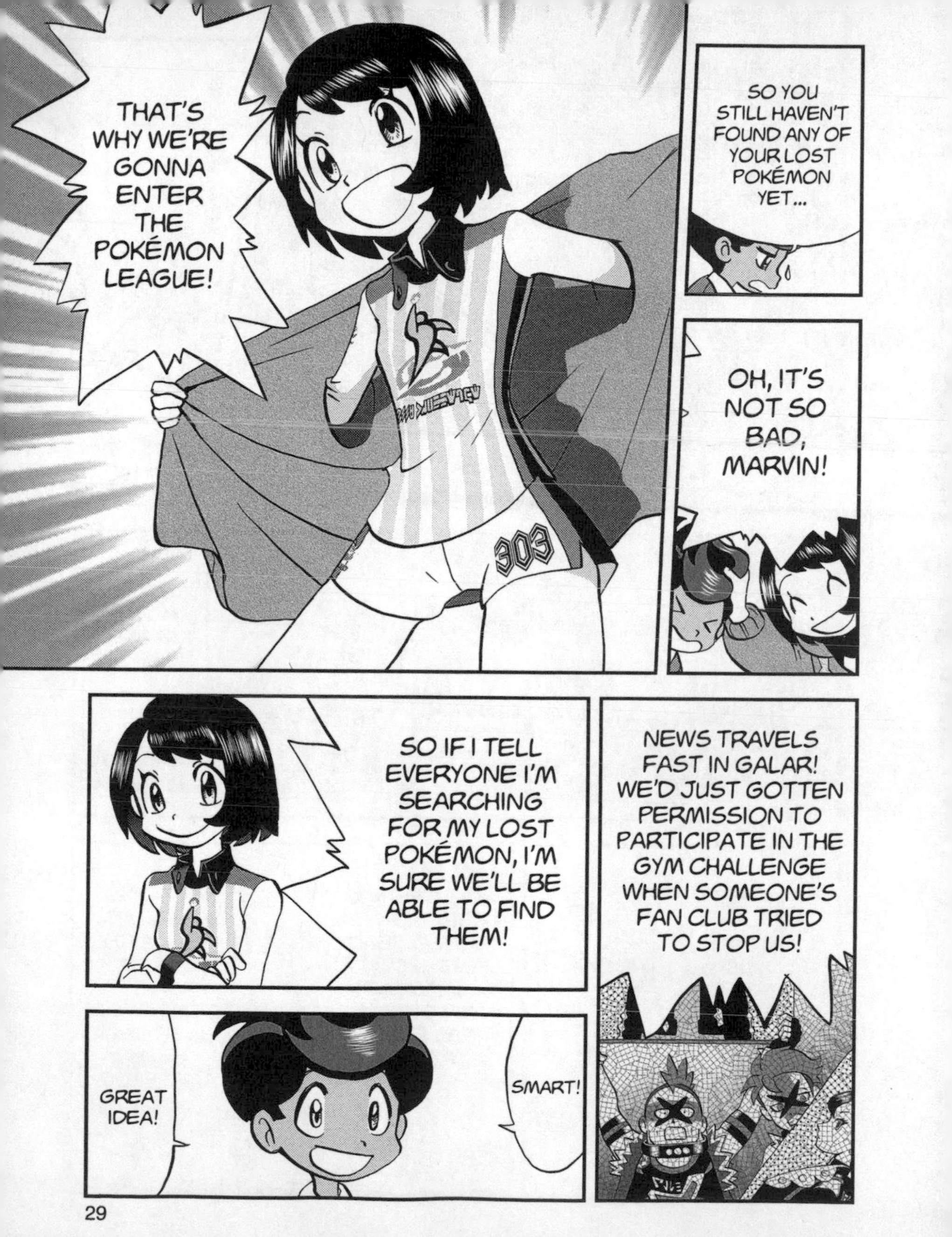
SO YOU STILL HAVEN'T FOUND ANY OF YOUR LOST POKéMON YET...
OH, IT'S NOT SO BAD, MARVIN!
THAT'S WHY WE'RE GONNA ENTER THE POKéMON LEAGUE!
NEWS TRAVELS FAST IN GALAR! WE'D JUST GOTTEN PERMISSION TO PARTICIPATE IN THE GYM CHALLENGE WHEN SOMEONE'S FAN CLUB TRIED TO STOP US!
SO IF I TELL EVERYONE I'M SEARCHING FOR MY LOST POKéMON, I'M SURE WE'LL BE ABLE TO FIND THEM!
SMART!
GREAT IDEA!

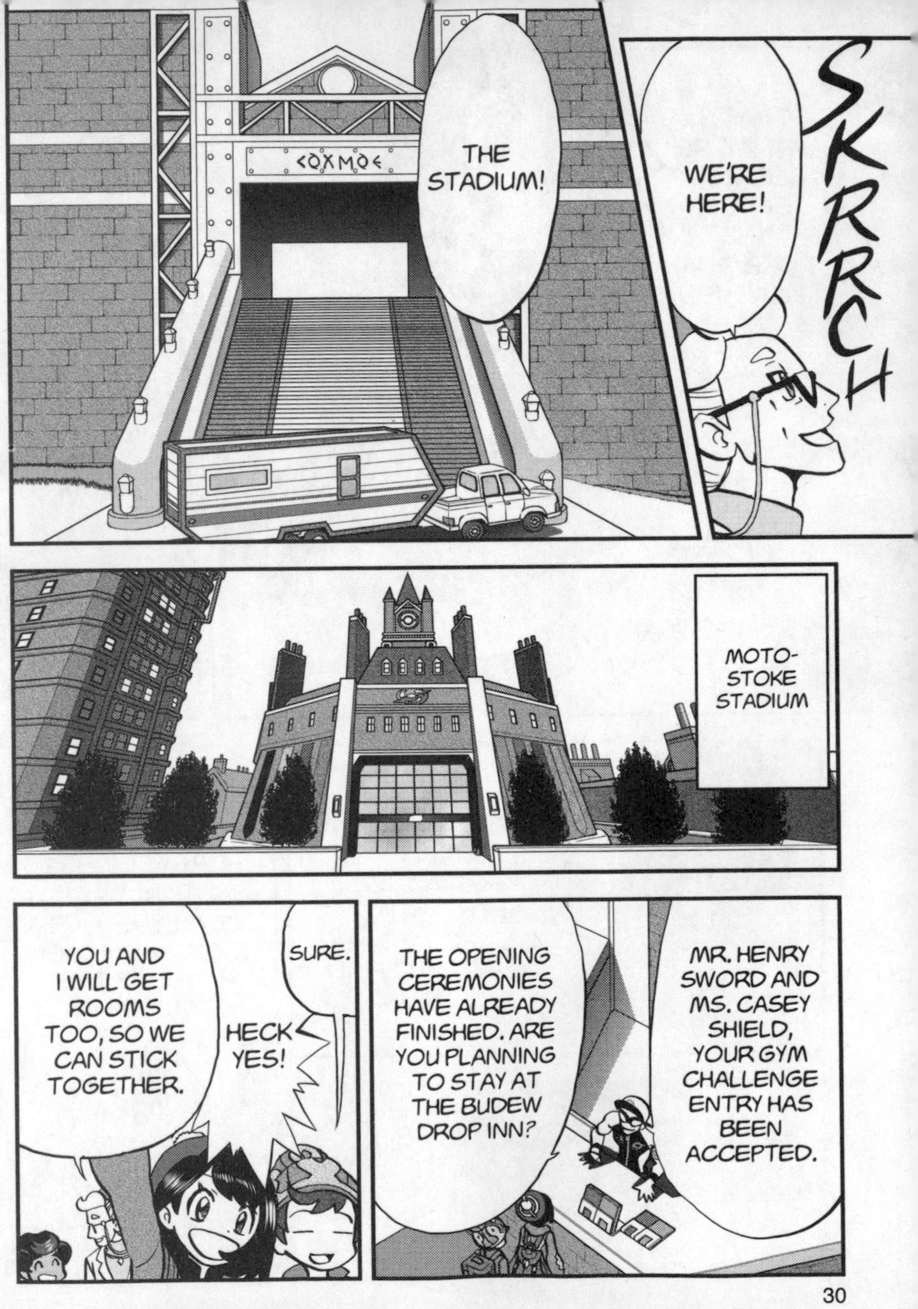
WE'RE HERE!
SKRRCH
THE STADIUM!
MOTO-STOKE STADIUM
MR. HENRY SWORD AND MS. CASEY SHIELD, YOUR GYM CHALLENGE ENTRY HAS BEEN ACCEPTED.
THE OPENING CEREMONIES HAVE ALREADY FINISHED. ARE YOU PLANNING TO STAY AT THE BUDEW DROP INN?
SURE.
YOU AND I WILL GET ROOMS TOO, SO WE CAN STICK TOGETHER.
HECK YES!

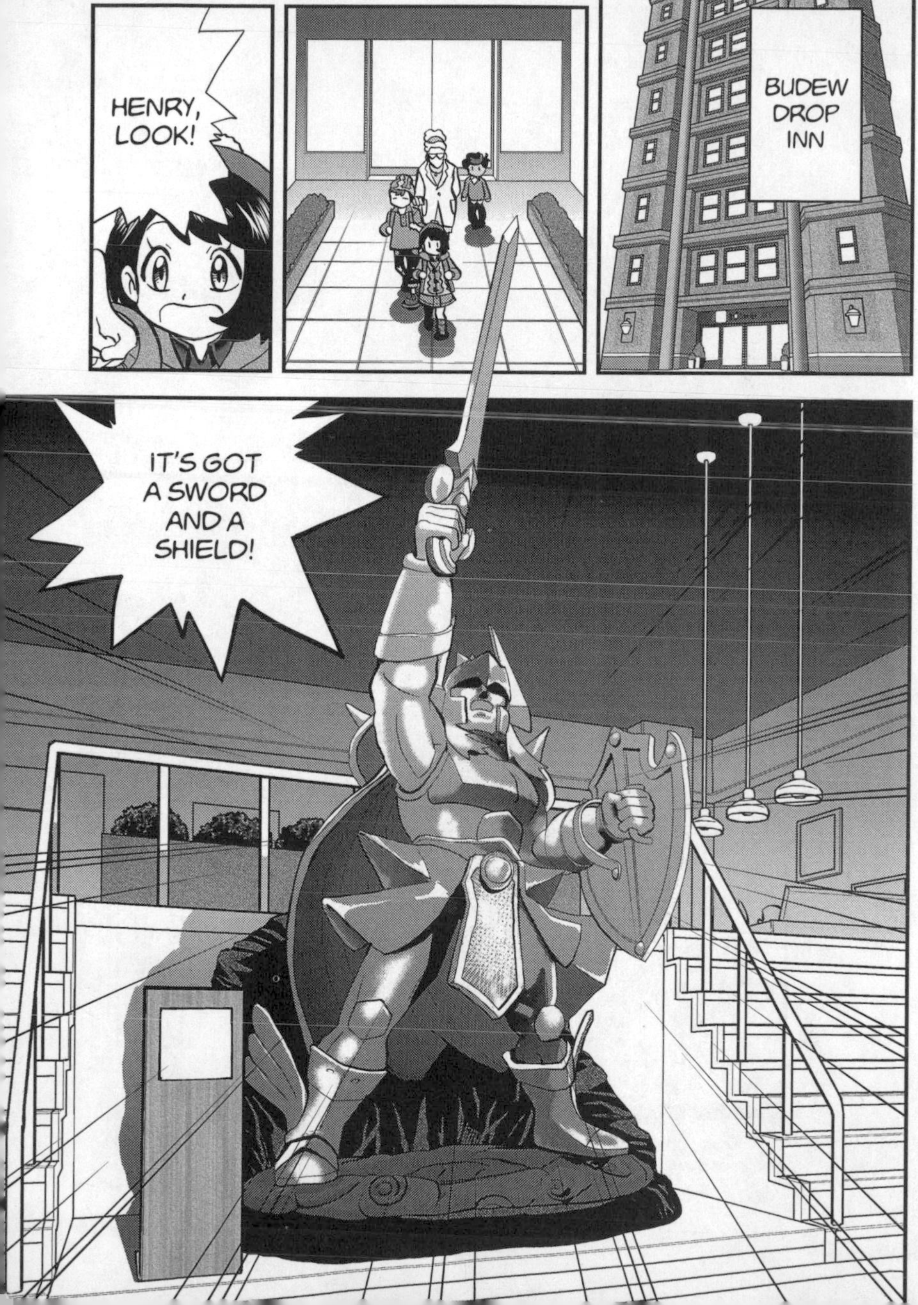
BUDEW DROP INN
HENRY, LOOK!
IT'S GOT A SWORD AND A SHIELD!

THE SECRETS OF DYNAMAX, PART 5

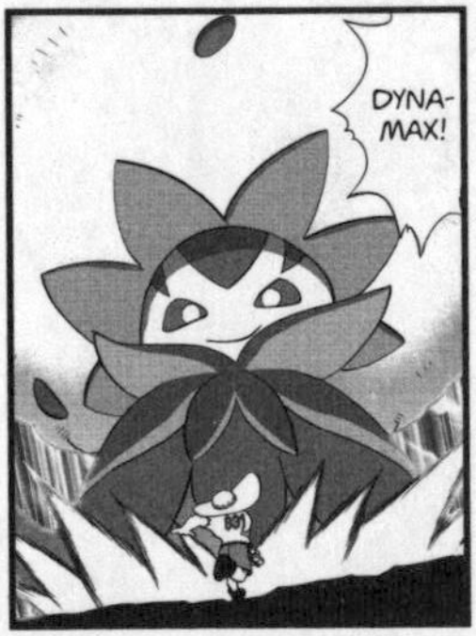
DYNA-
MAX!

▲ A strong opponent becomes even stronger!

Stadium

The Wild Area isn't the only place with Power Spots. The stadiums of Galar have all been built on Power Spots, so everyone can Dynamax their Pokémon during a Gym battle.

Adventure 6 Watch Out!! Strong Rivals

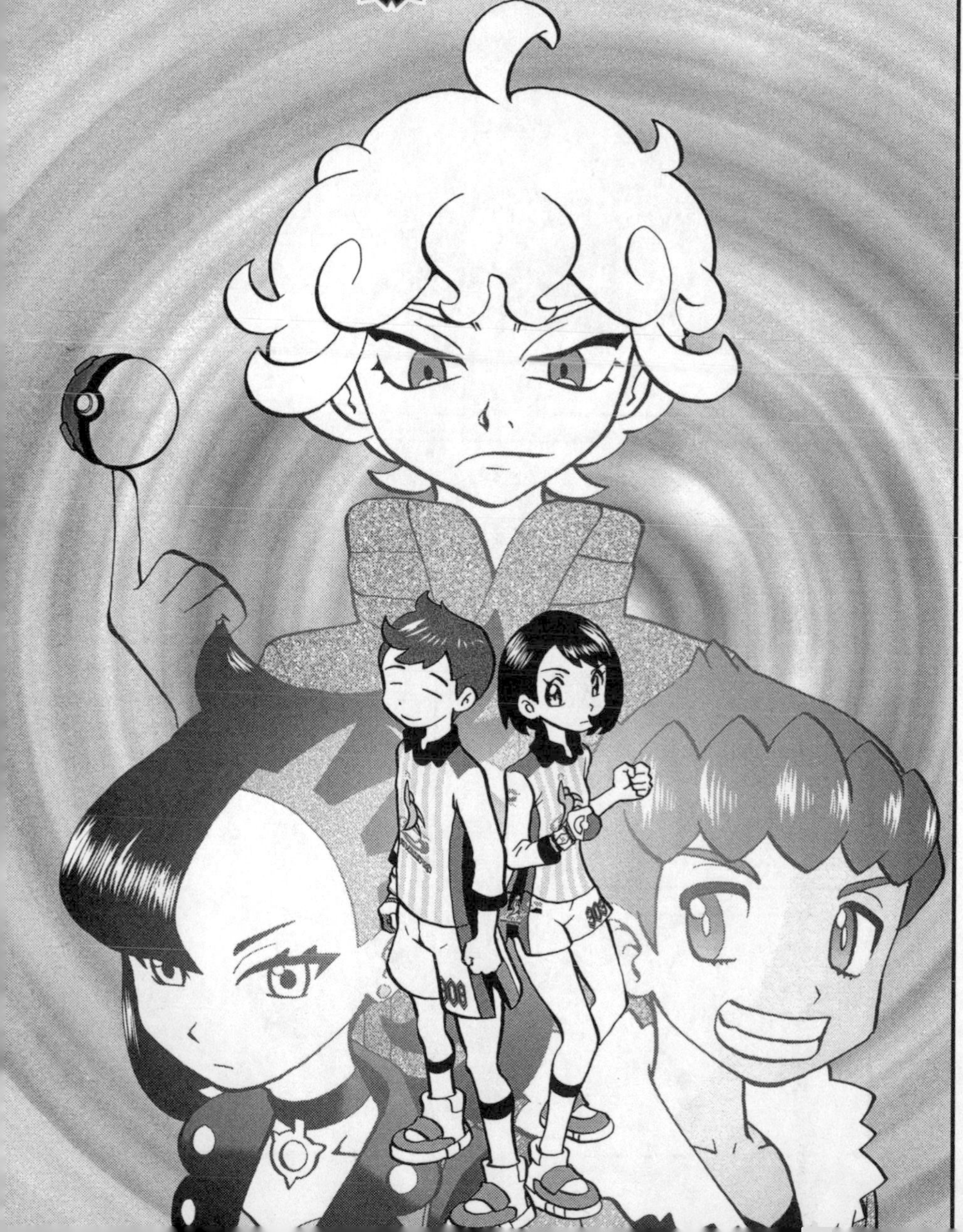

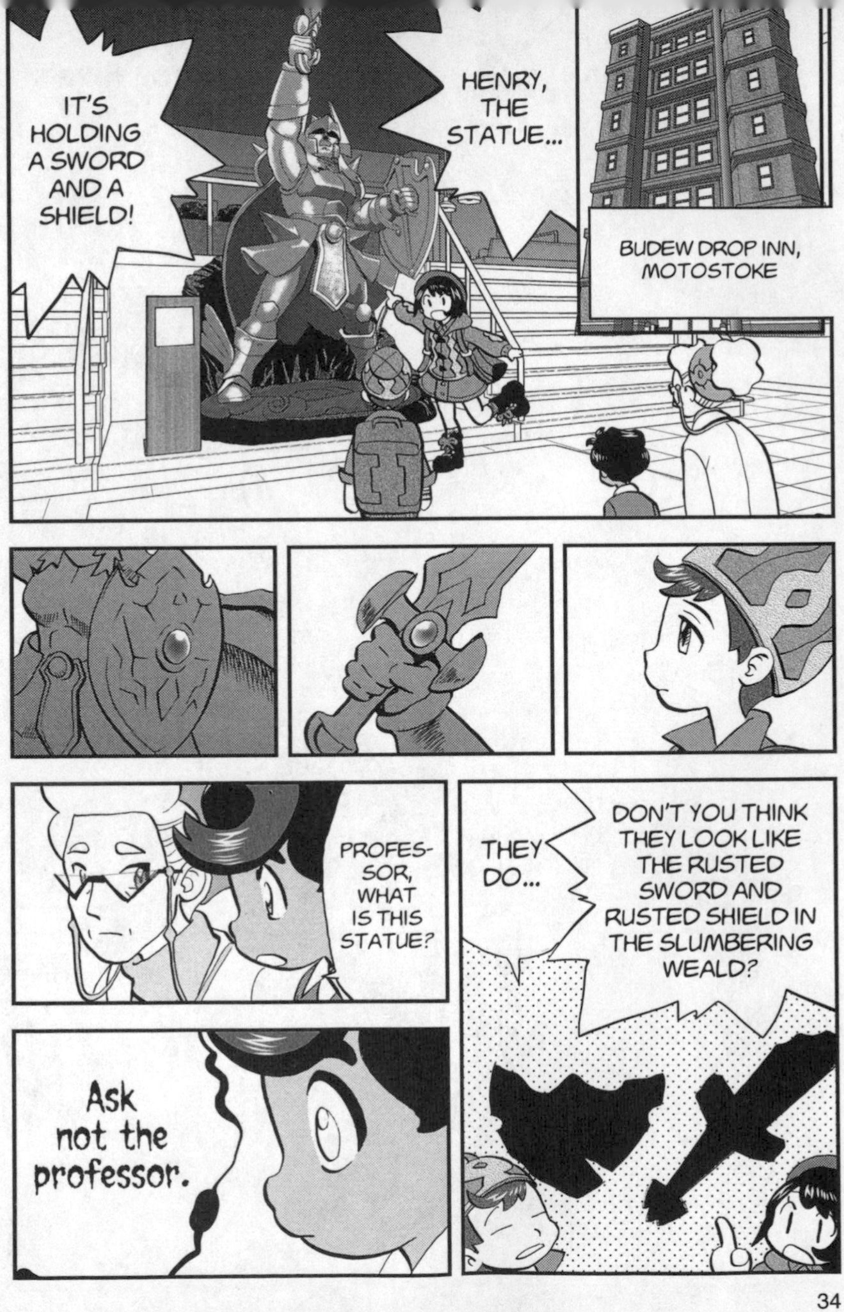
BUDEW DROP INN, MOTOSTOKE
HENRY, THE STATUE...
IT'S HOLDING A SWORD AND A SHIELD!
DON'T YOU THINK THEY LOOK LIKE THE RUSTED SWORD AND RUSTED SHIELD IN THE SLUMBERING WEALD?
THEY DO...
PROFESSOR, WHAT IS THIS STATUE?
Ask not the professor.

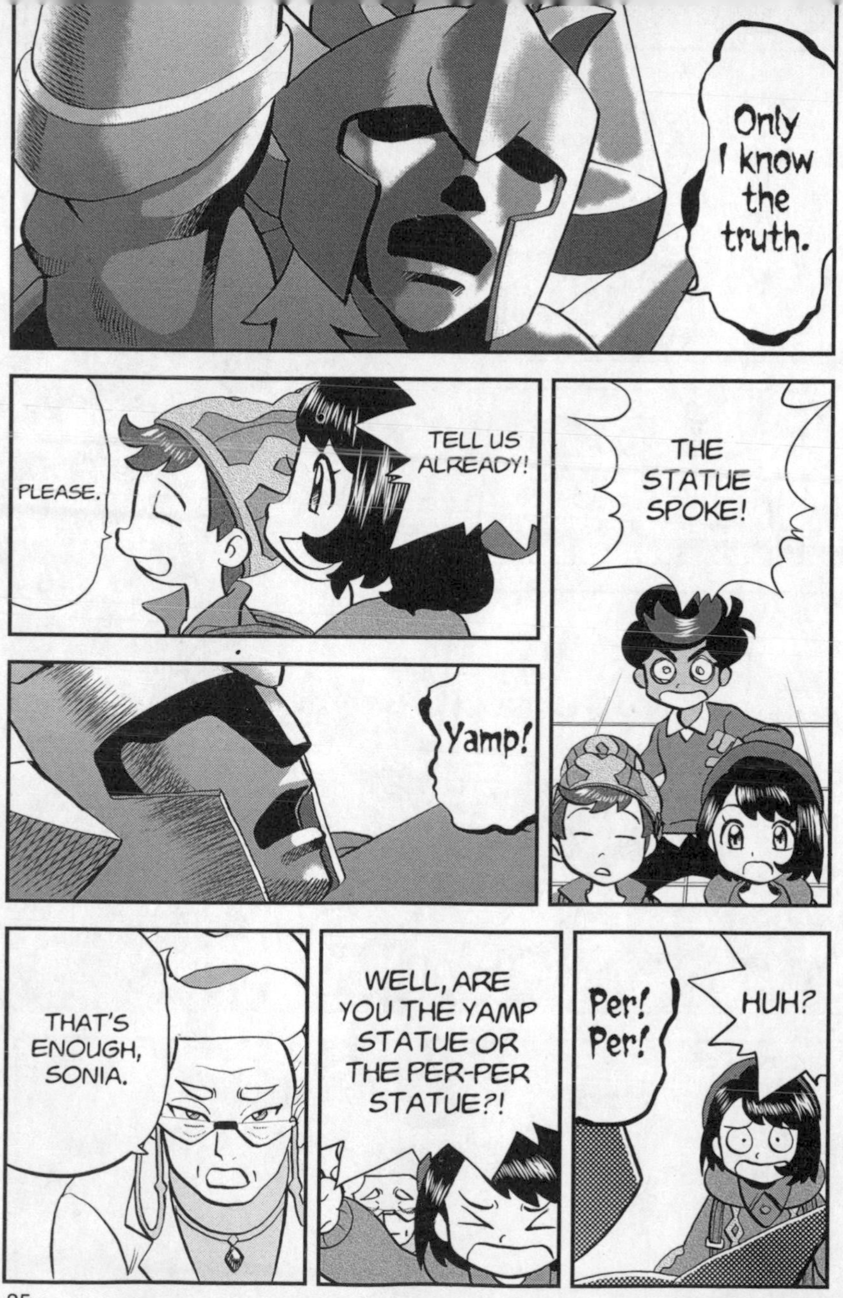
Only I know the truth.
THE STATUE SPOKE!
TELL US ALREADY!
PLEASE.
Yamp!
HUH?
Per! Per!
WELL, ARE YOU THE YAMP STATUE OR THE PER-PER STATUE?!
THAT'S ENOUGH, SONIA.

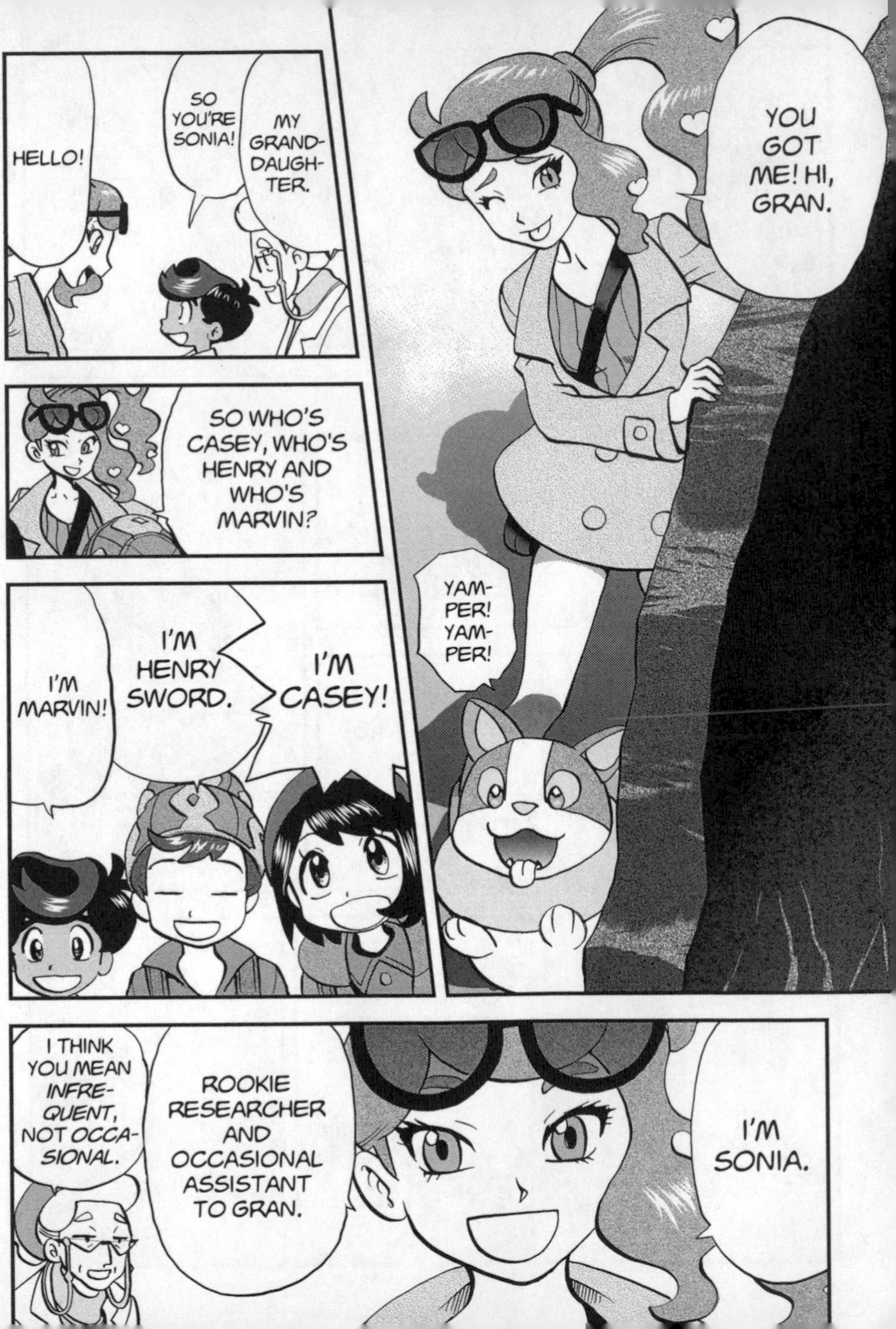
YOU GOT ME! HI, GRAN.
YAMPER! YAMPER!
MY GRANDDAUGHTER.
SO YOU'RE SONIA!
HELLO!
SO WHO'S CASEY, WHO'S HENRY AND WHO'S MARVIN?
I'M CASEY!
I'M HENRY SWORD.
I'M MARVIN!
I'M SONIA.
ROOKIE RESEARCHER AND OCCASIONAL ASSISTANT TO GRAN.
I THINK YOU MEAN *INFREQUENT*, NOT *OCCASIONAL*.

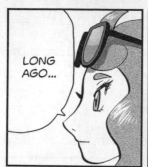

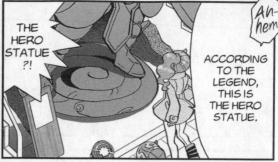

Ah-hem.
ACCORDING TO THE LEGEND, THIS IS THE HERO STATUE.
THE HERO STATUE ?!
LONG AGO...
...A BLACK STORM COVERED THE GALAR REGION.
PEOPLE CALLED IT THE DARKEST DAY.
POKéMON EVERY-WHERE SUDDENLY TURNED GIGANTIC...
...AND BEGAN TO ASSAULT THE LAND.

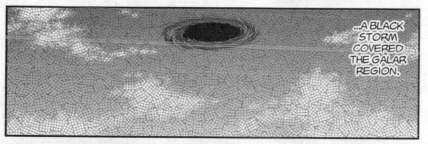

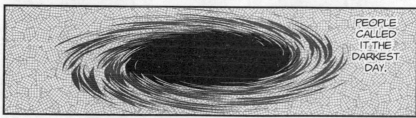

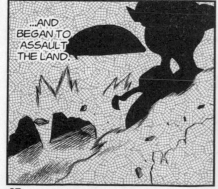

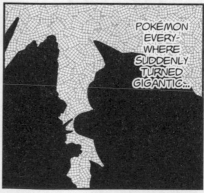

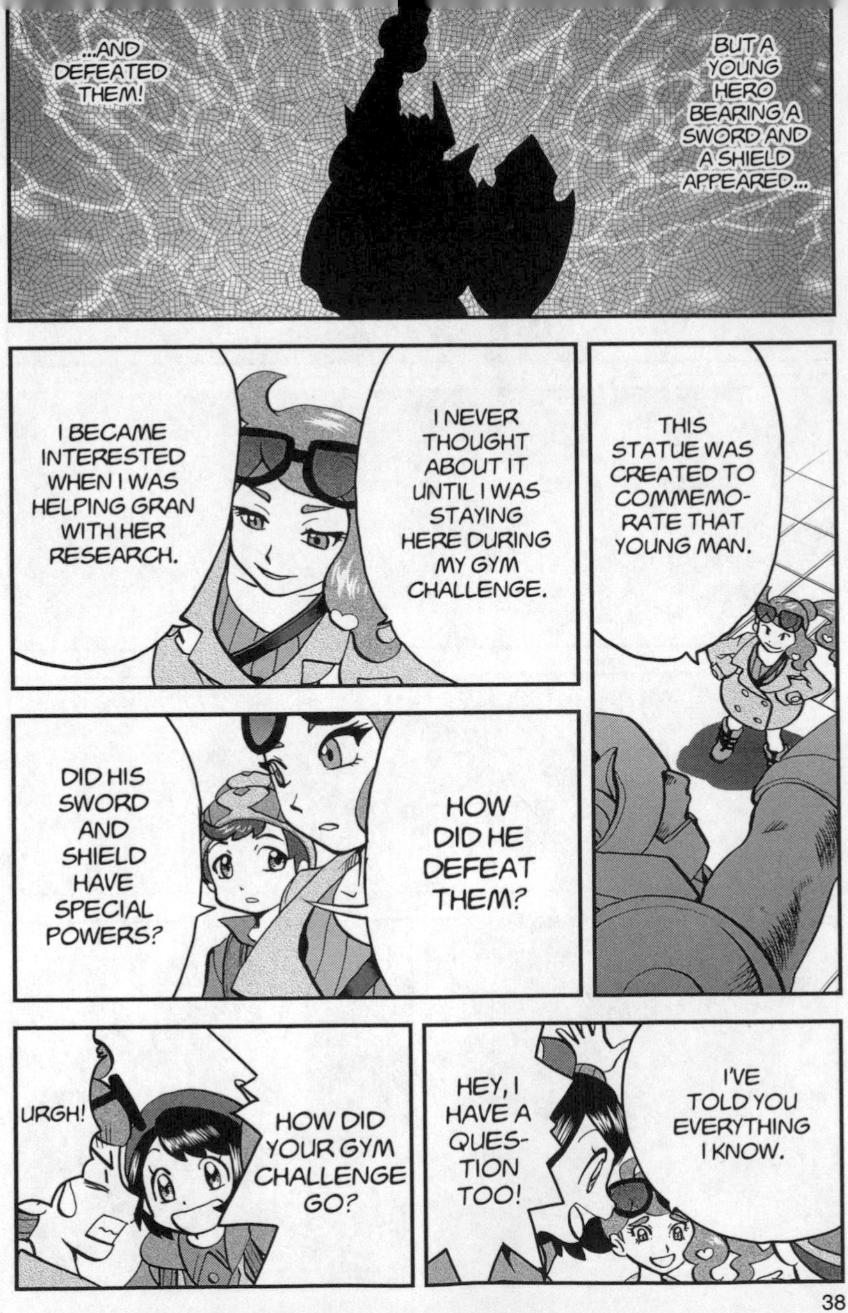
BUT A YOUNG HERO BEARING A SWORD AND A SHIELD APPEARED...
...AND DEFEATED THEM!
THIS STATUE WAS CREATED TO COMMEMO-RATE THAT YOUNG MAN.
I NEVER THOUGHT ABOUT IT UNTIL I WAS STAYING HERE DURING MY GYM CHALLENGE.
I BECAME INTERESTED WHEN I WAS HELPING GRAN WITH HER RESEARCH.
HOW DID HE DEFEAT THEM?
DID HIS SWORD AND SHIELD HAVE SPECIAL POWERS?
I'VE TOLD YOU EVERYTHING I KNOW.
HEY, I HAVE A QUES-TION TOO!
HOW DID YOUR GYM CHALLENGE GO?
URGH!

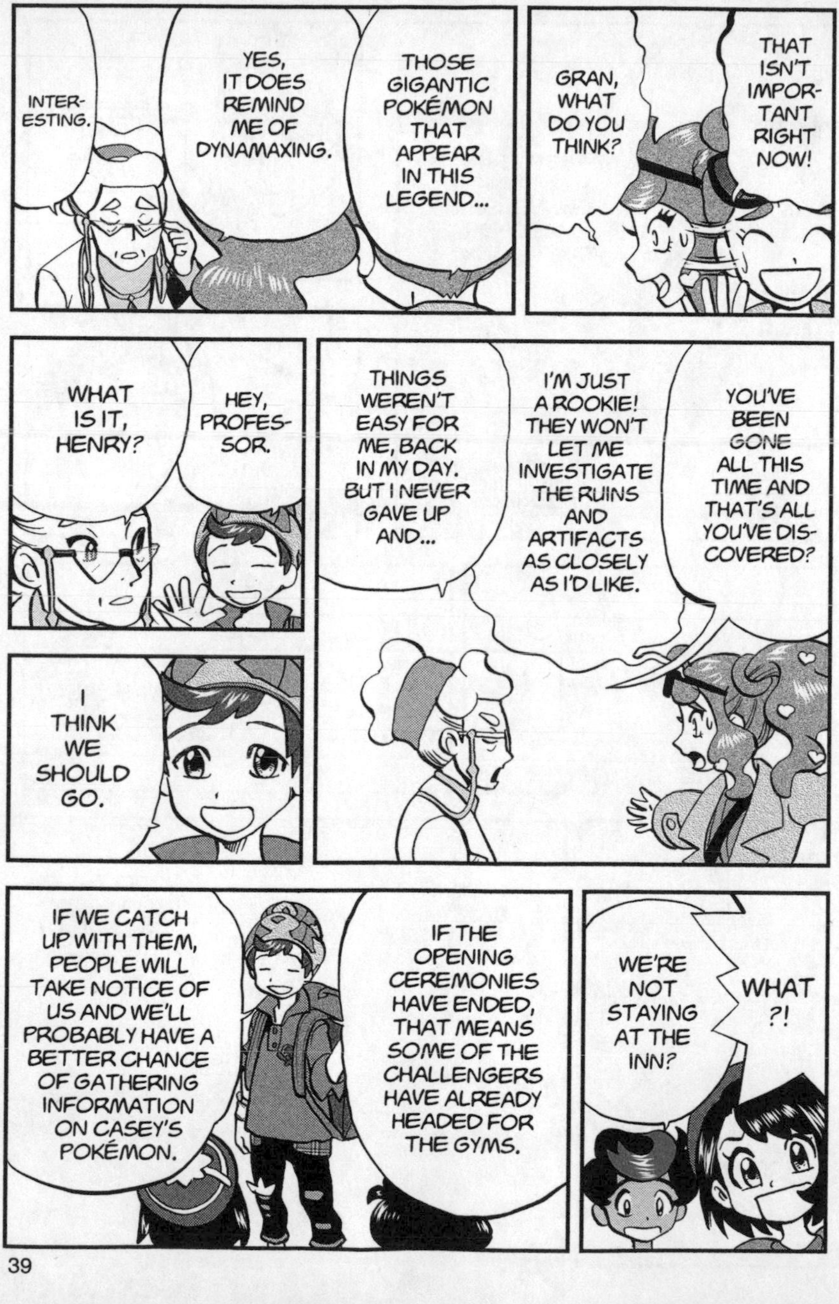
THAT ISN'T IMPOR-TANT RIGHT NOW!
GRAN, WHAT DO YOU THINK?
THOSE GIGANTIC POKÉMON THAT APPEAR IN THIS LEGEND...
YES, IT DOES REMIND ME OF DYNAMAXING.
INTER-ESTING.
YOU'VE BEEN GONE ALL THIS TIME AND THAT'S ALL YOU'VE DIS-COVERED?
I'M JUST A ROOKIE! THEY WON'T LET ME INVESTIGATE THE RUINS AND ARTIFACTS AS CLOSELY AS I'D LIKE.
THINGS WEREN'T EASY FOR ME, BACK IN MY DAY. BUT I NEVER GAVE UP AND...
HEY, PROFES-SOR.
WHAT IS IT, HENRY?
I THINK WE SHOULD GO.
WHAT ?!
WE'RE NOT STAYING AT THE INN?
IF THE OPENING CEREMONIES HAVE ENDED, THAT MEANS SOME OF THE CHALLENGERS HAVE ALREADY HEADED FOR THE GYMS.
IF WE CATCH UP WITH THEM, PEOPLE WILL TAKE NOTICE OF US AND WE'LL PROBABLY HAVE A BETTER CHANCE OF GATHERING INFORMATION ON CASEY'S POKÉMON.

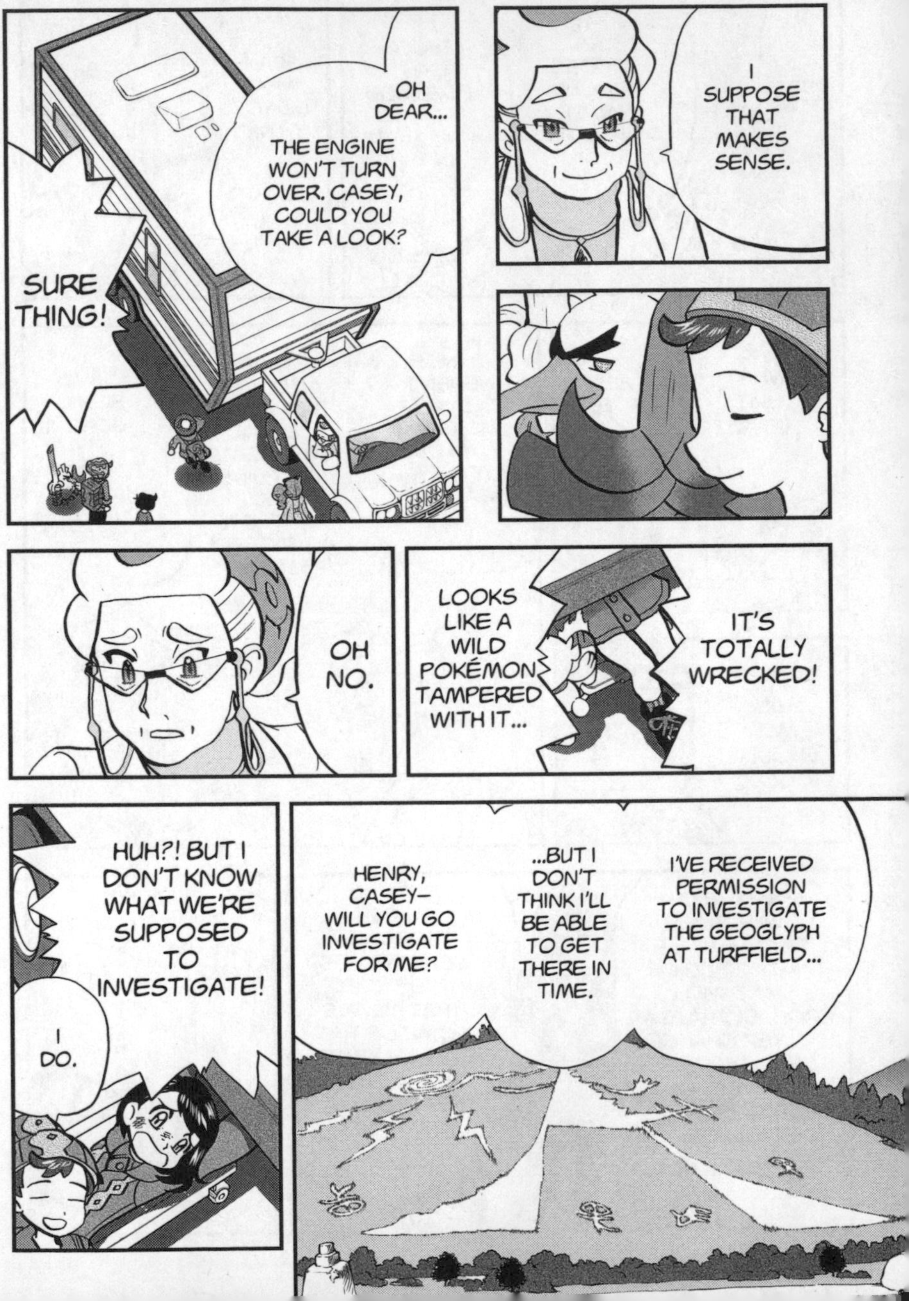
I SUPPOSE THAT MAKES SENSE.
OH DEAR...
THE ENGINE WON'T TURN OVER. CASEY, COULD YOU TAKE A LOOK?
SURE THING!
IT'S TOTALLY WRECKED!
LOOKS LIKE A WILD POKÉMON TAMPERED WITH IT...
OH NO.
I'VE RECEIVED PERMISSION TO INVESTIGATE THE GEOGLYPH AT TURFFIELD...
...BUT I DON'T THINK I'LL BE ABLE TO GET THERE IN TIME.
HENRY, CASEY— WILL YOU GO INVESTIGATE FOR ME?
HUH?! BUT I DON'T KNOW WHAT WE'RE SUPPOSED TO INVESTIGATE!
I DO.

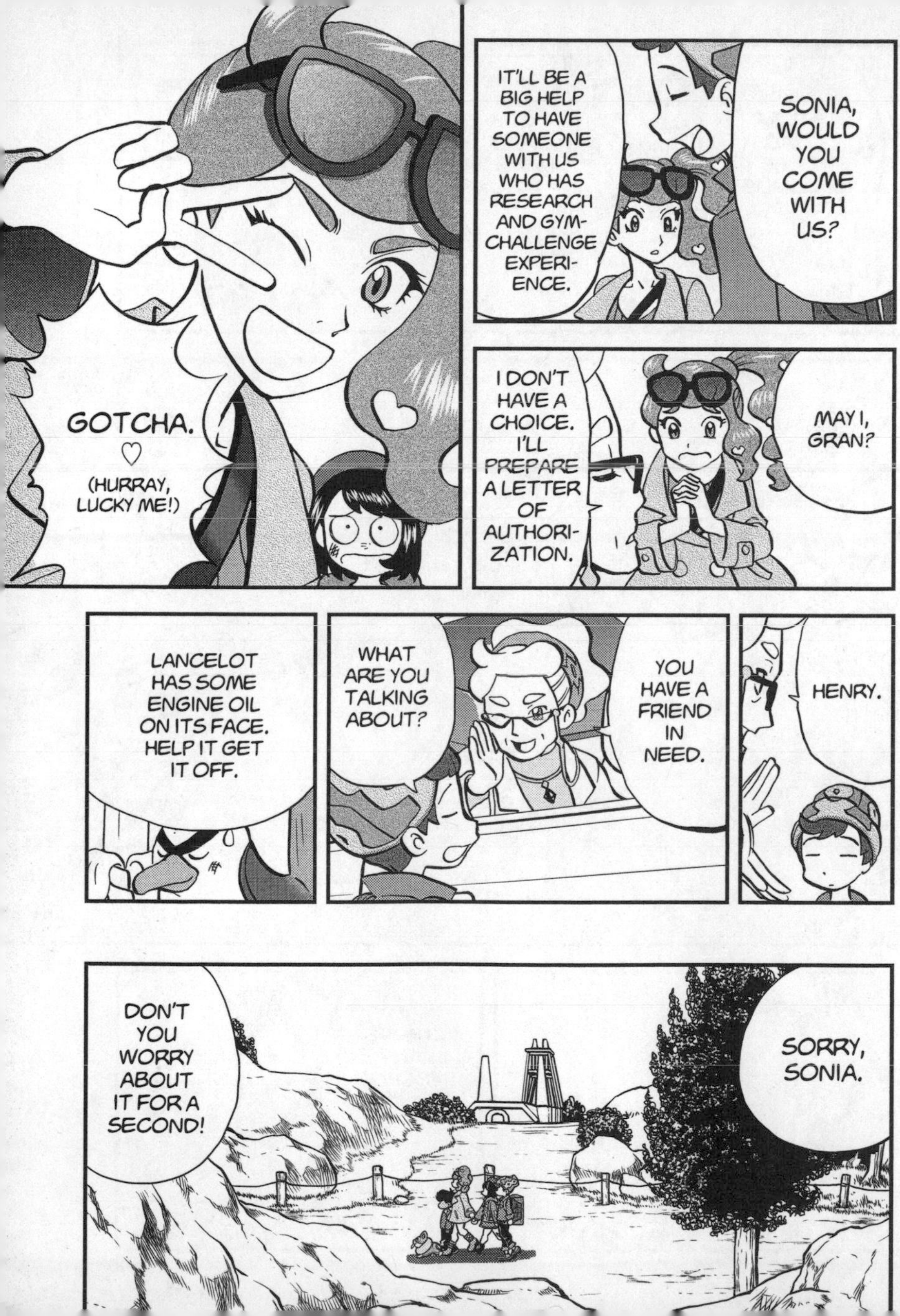
SONIA, WOULD YOU COME WITH US?
IT'LL BE A BIG HELP TO HAVE SOMEONE WITH US WHO HAS RESEARCH AND GYM-CHALLENGE EXPERIENCE.
MAY I, GRAN?
I DON'T HAVE A CHOICE. I'LL PREPARE A LETTER OF AUTHORIZATION.
GOTCHA. ♡
(HURRAY, LUCKY ME!)
HENRY.
YOU HAVE A FRIEND IN NEED.
WHAT ARE YOU TALKING ABOUT?
LANCELOT HAS SOME ENGINE OIL ON ITS FACE. HELP IT GET IT OFF.
SORRY, SONIA.
DON'T YOU WORRY ABOUT IT FOR A SECOND!

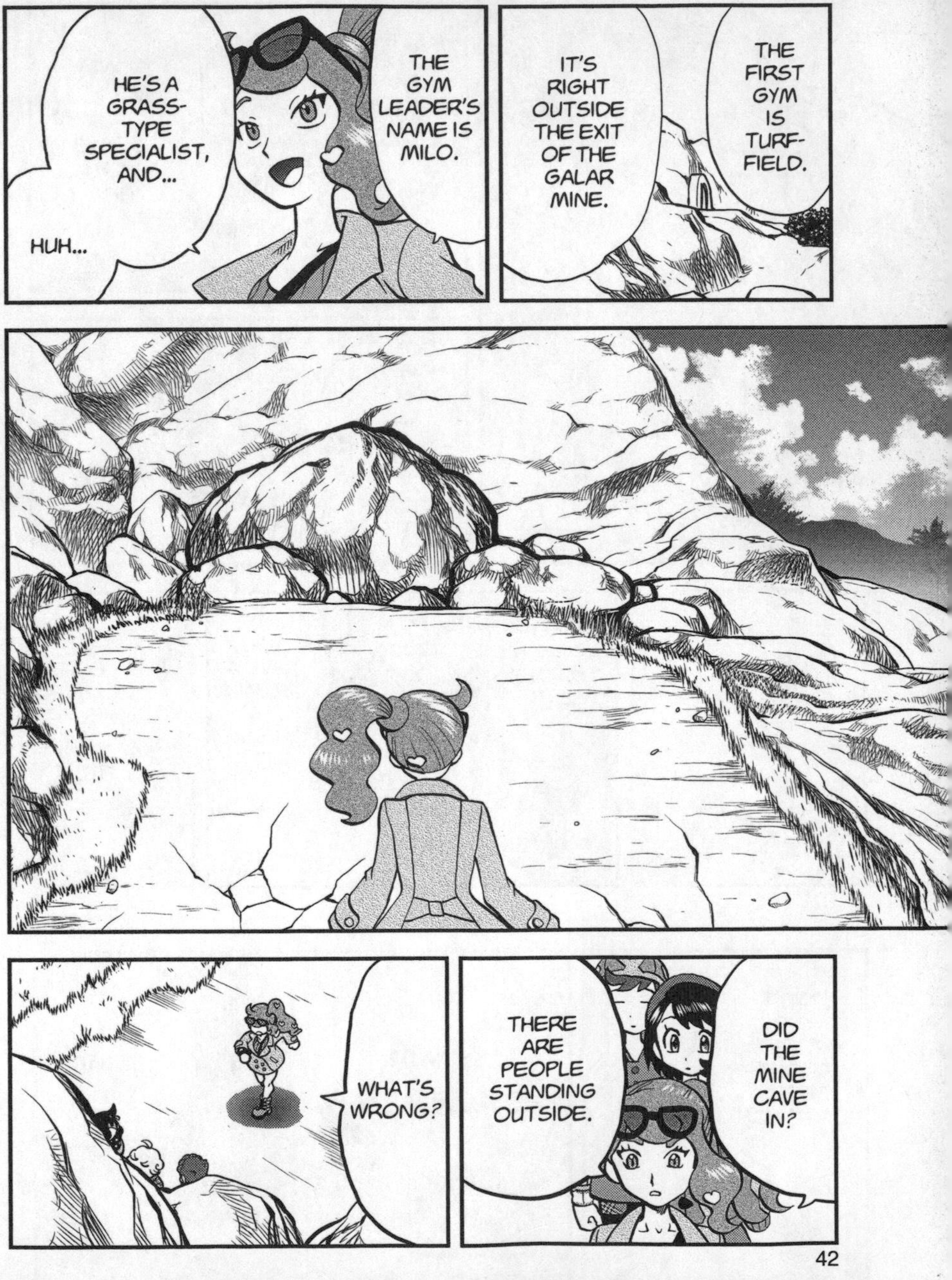
THE FIRST GYM IS TURF-FIELD.
IT'S RIGHT OUTSIDE THE EXIT OF THE GALAR MINE.
THE GYM LEADER'S NAME IS MILO.
HE'S A GRASS-TYPE SPECIALIST, AND...
HUH...
DID THE MINE CAVE IN?
THERE ARE PEOPLE STANDING OUTSIDE.
WHAT'S WRONG?

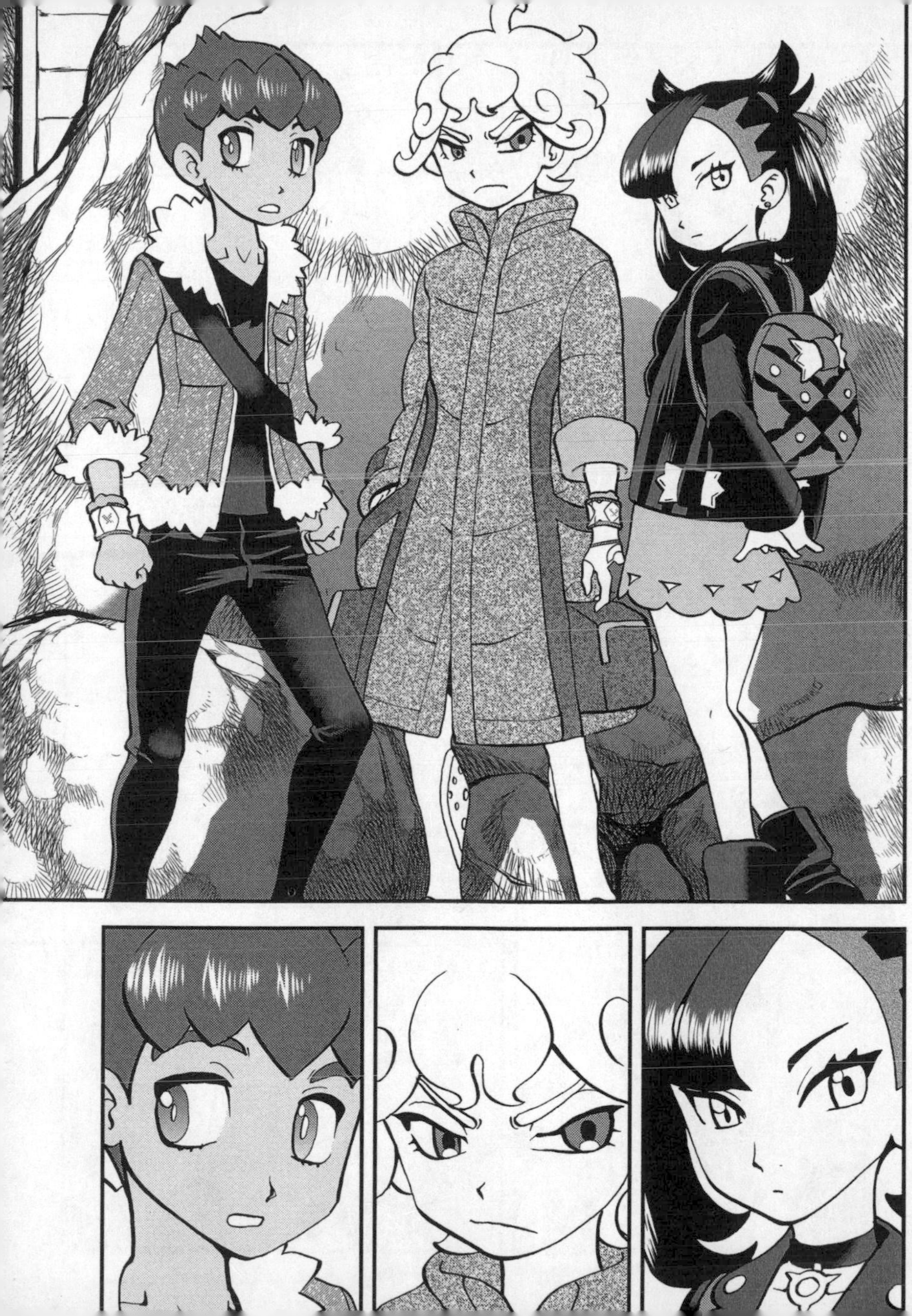

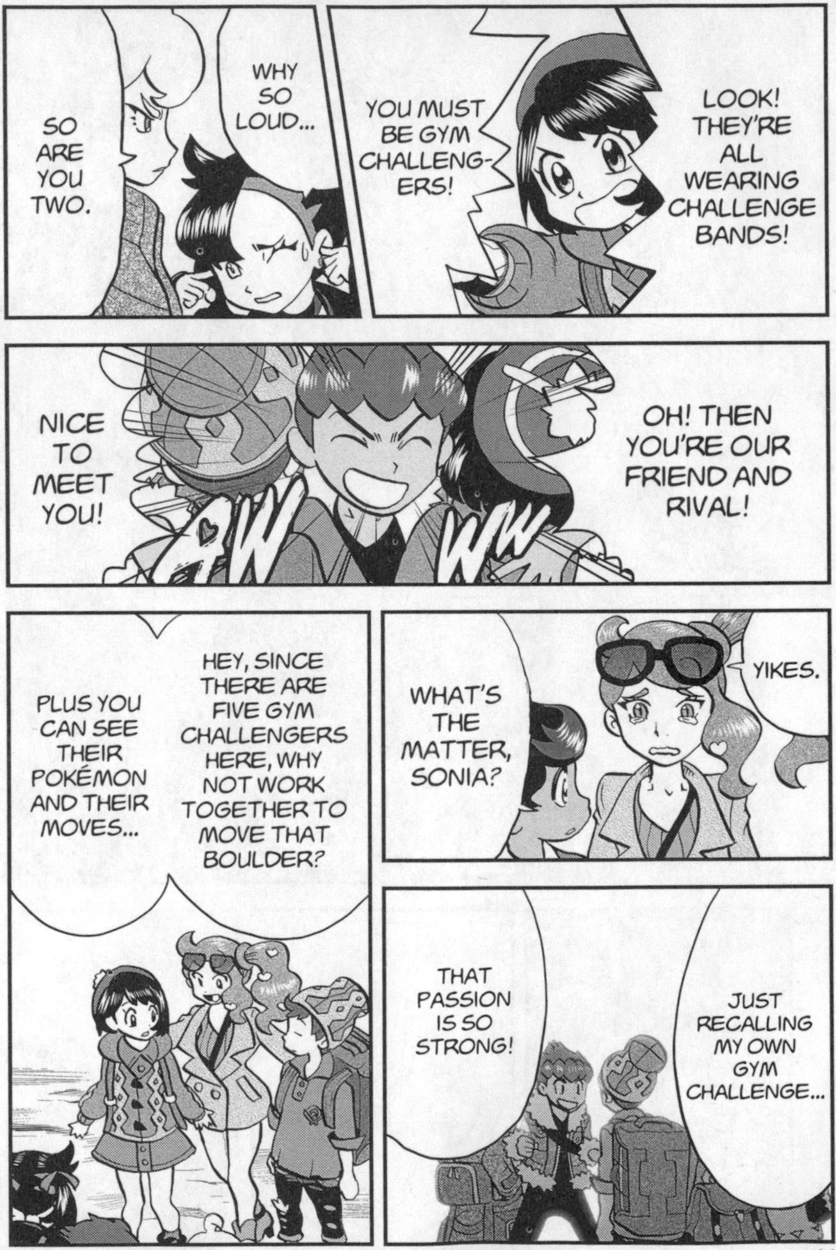
LOOK! THEY'RE ALL WEARING CHALLENGE BANDS!
YOU MUST BE GYM CHALLENG-ERS!
WHY SO LOUD...
SO ARE YOU TWO.
OH! THEN YOU'RE OUR FRIEND AND RIVAL!
NICE TO MEET YOU!
YIKES.
WHAT'S THE MATTER, SONIA?
JUST RECALLING MY OWN GYM CHALLENGE...
THAT PASSION IS SO STRONG!
HEY, SINCE THERE ARE FIVE GYM CHALLENGERS HERE, WHY NOT WORK TOGETHER TO MOVE THAT BOULDER?
PLUS YOU CAN SEE THEIR POKÉMON AND THEIR MOVES...

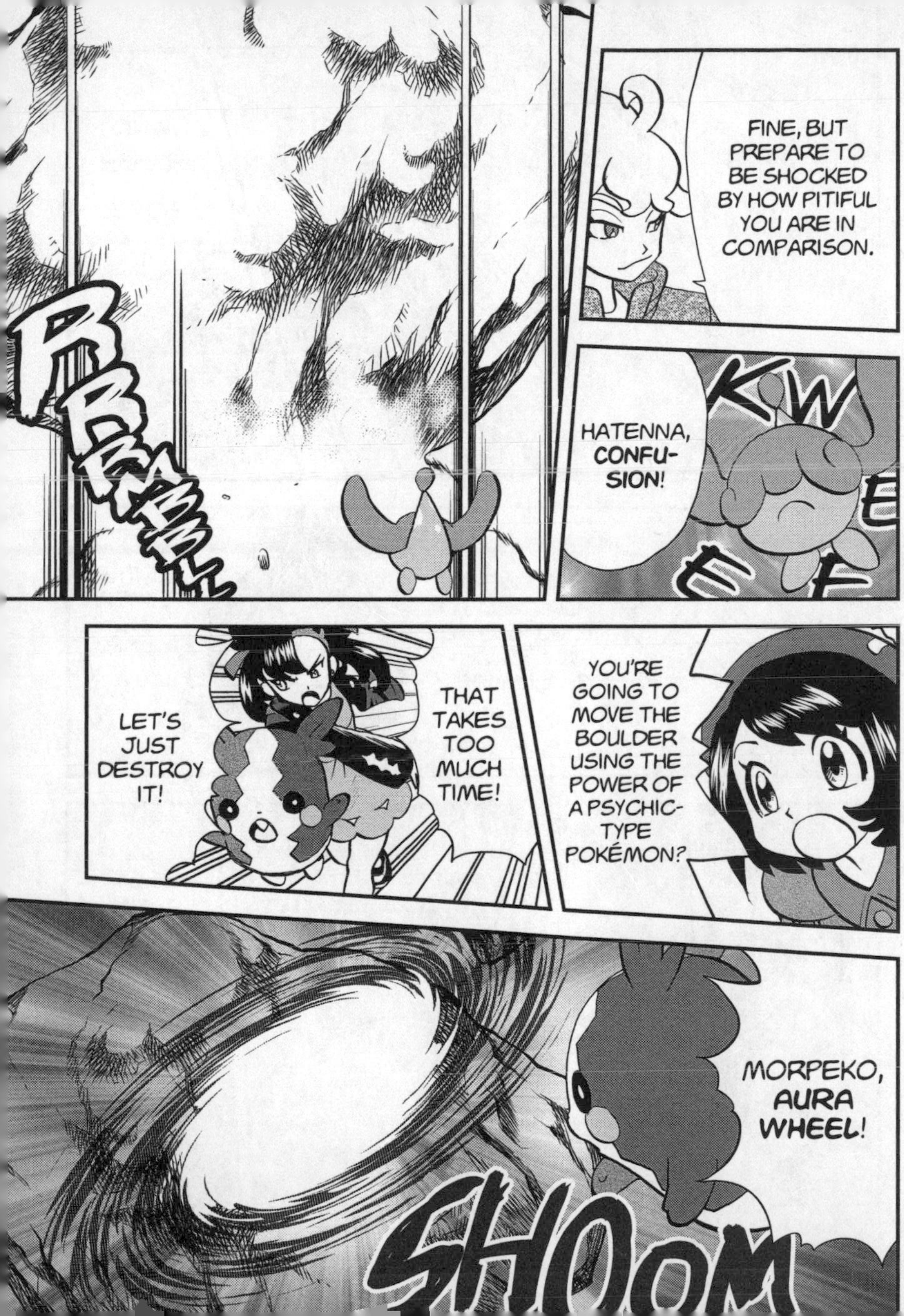
FINE, BUT PREPARE TO BE SHOCKED BY HOW PITIFUL YOU ARE IN COMPARISON.
HATENNA, CONFUSION!
KWEEE
RRRMBLL
YOU'RE GOING TO MOVE THE BOULDER USING THE POWER OF A PSYCHIC-TYPE POKÉMON?
THAT TAKES TOO MUCH TIME!
LET'S JUST DESTROY IT!
MORPEKO, AURA WHEEL!
SHOOM

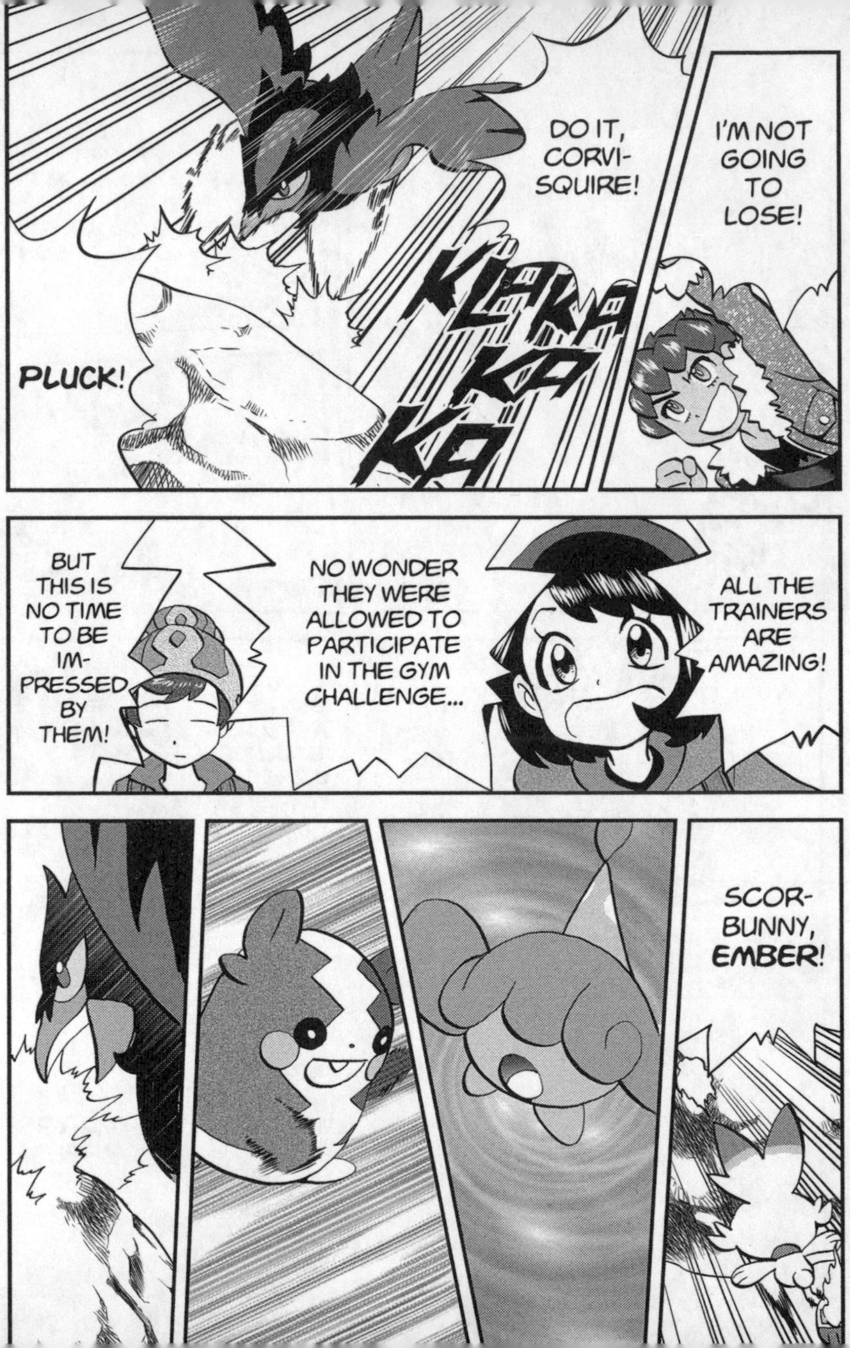
I'M NOT GOING TO LOSE!
DO IT, CORVI- SQUIRE!
PLUCK!
ALL THE TRAINERS ARE AMAZING!
NO WONDER THEY WERE ALLOWED TO PARTICIPATE IN THE GYM CHALLENGE...
BUT THIS IS NO TIME TO BE IM- PRESSED BY THEM!
SCOR- BUNNY, EMBER!

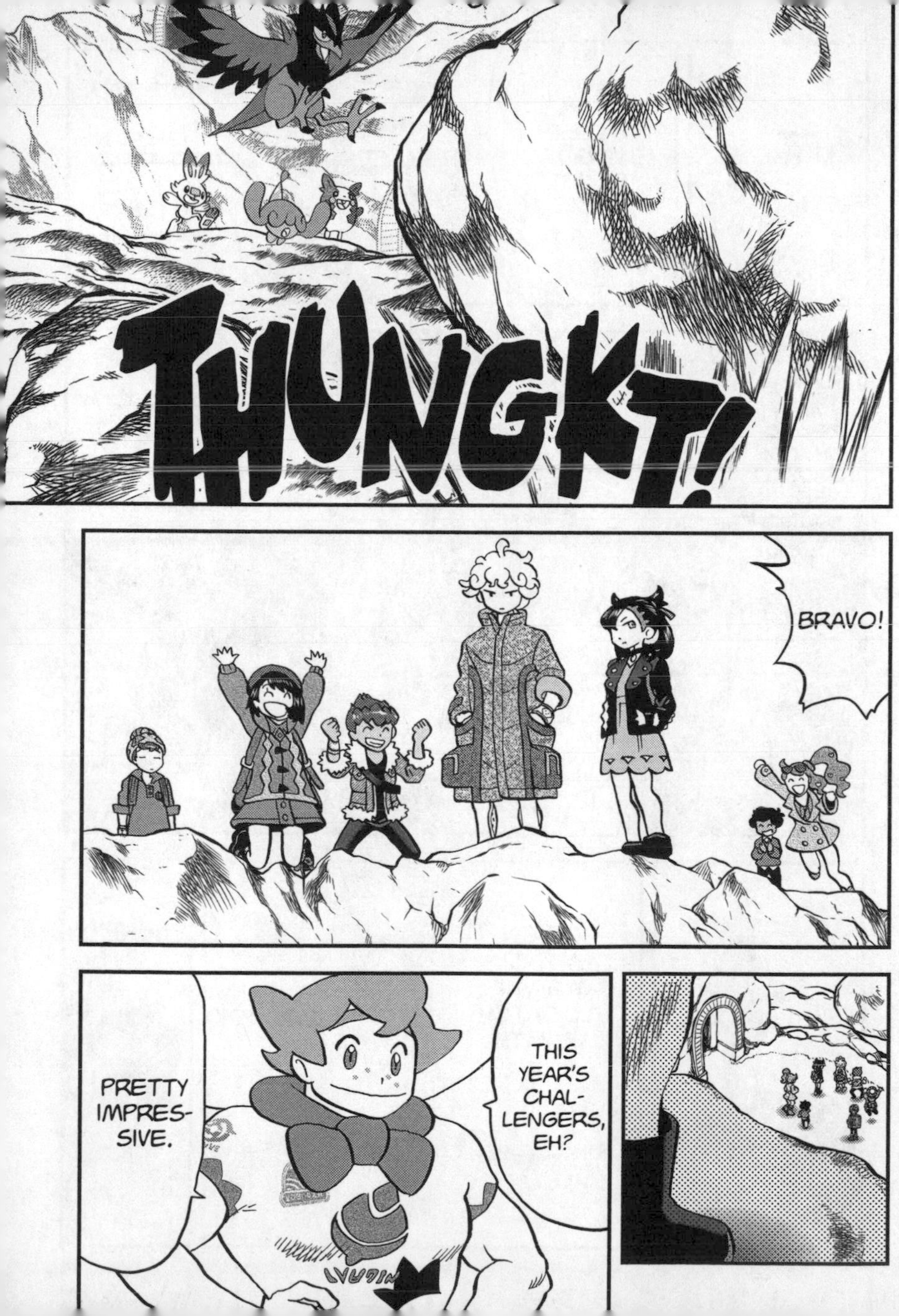
THUNGKT!
BRAVO!
THIS YEAR'S CHAL-LENGERS, EH?
PRETTY IMPRES-SIVE.

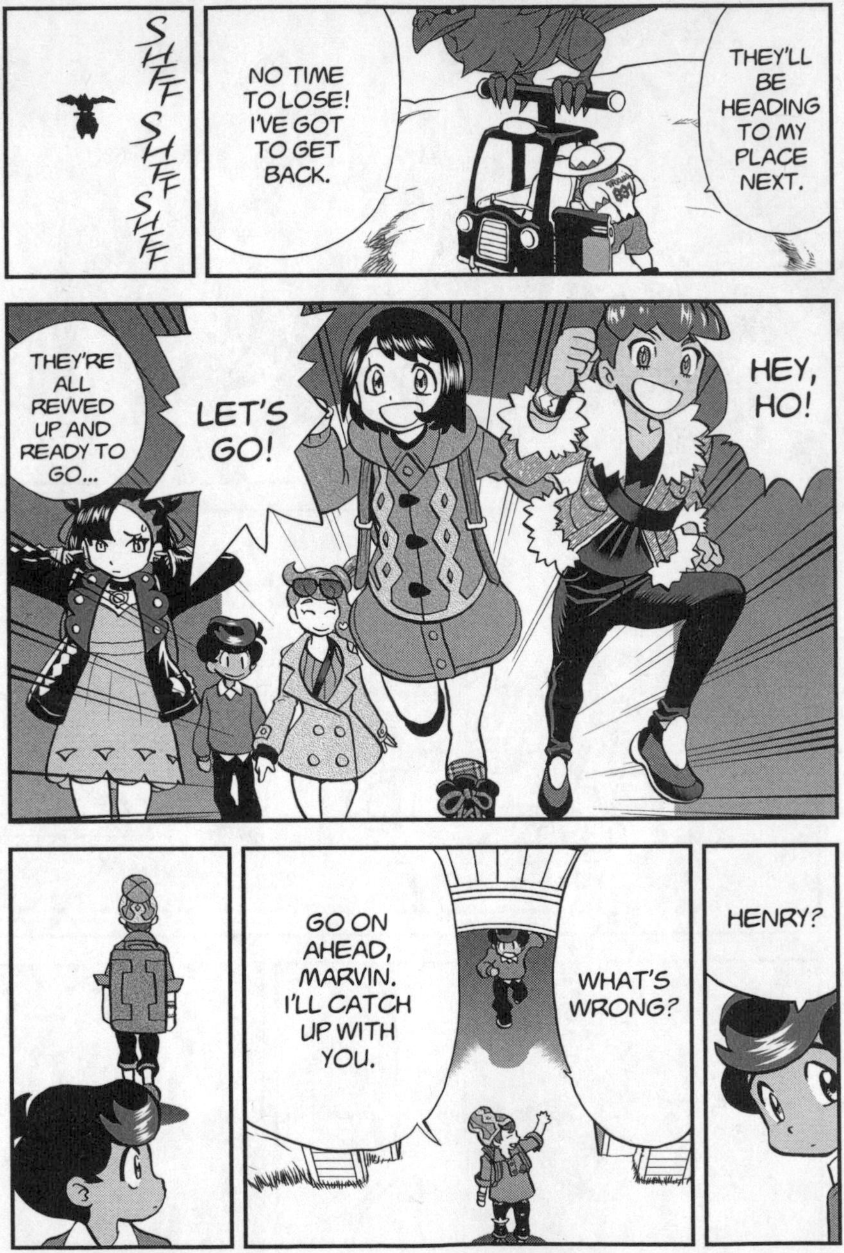
THEY'LL BE HEADING TO MY PLACE NEXT.
NO TIME TO LOSE! I'VE GOT TO GET BACK.
SHFF SHFF SHFF
HEY, HO!
LET'S GO!
THEY'RE ALL REVVED UP AND READY TO GO...
HENRY?
WHAT'S WRONG?
GO ON AHEAD, MARVIN. I'LL CATCH UP WITH YOU.

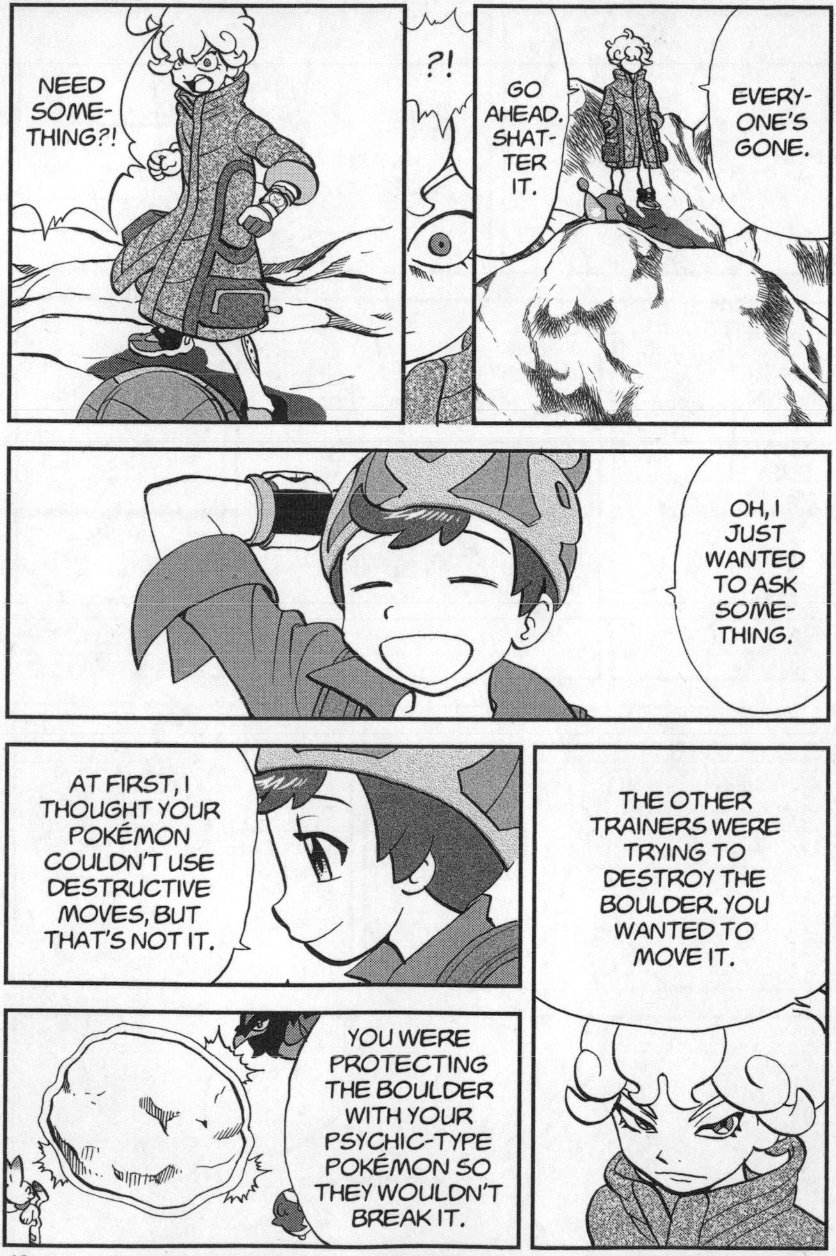
EVERY-ONE'S GONE.
GO AHEAD. SHAT-TER IT.
?!
NEED SOME-THING?!
OH, I JUST WANTED TO ASK SOME-THING.
THE OTHER TRAINERS WERE TRYING TO DESTROY THE BOULDER. YOU WANTED TO MOVE IT.
AT FIRST, I THOUGHT YOUR POKÉMON COULDN'T USE DESTRUCTIVE MOVES, BUT THAT'S NOT IT.
YOU WERE PROTECTING THE BOULDER WITH YOUR PSYCHIC-TYPE POKÉMON SO THEY WOULDN'T BREAK IT.

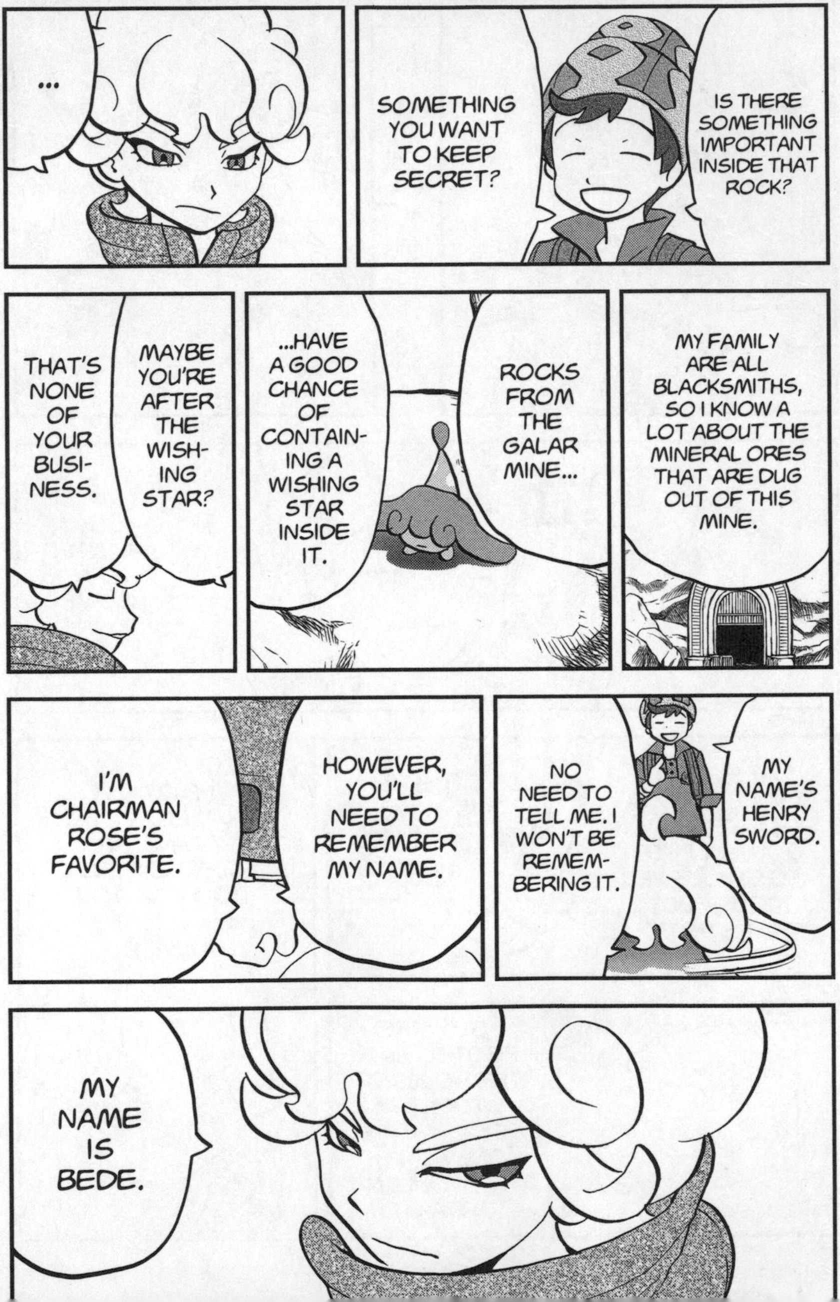
IS THERE SOMETHING IMPORTANT INSIDE THAT ROCK?
SOMETHING YOU WANT TO KEEP SECRET?
...
MY FAMILY ARE ALL BLACKSMITHS, SO I KNOW A LOT ABOUT THE MINERAL ORES THAT ARE DUG OUT OF THIS MINE.
ROCKS FROM THE GALAR MINE...
...HAVE A GOOD CHANCE OF CONTAINING A WISHING STAR INSIDE IT.
MAYBE YOU'RE AFTER THE WISHING STAR?
THAT'S NONE OF YOUR BUSINESS.
MY NAME'S HENRY SWORD.
NO NEED TO TELL ME. I WON'T BE REMEMBERING IT.
HOWEVER, YOU'LL NEED TO REMEMBER MY NAME.
I'M CHAIRMAN ROSE'S FAVORITE.
MY NAME IS BEDE.

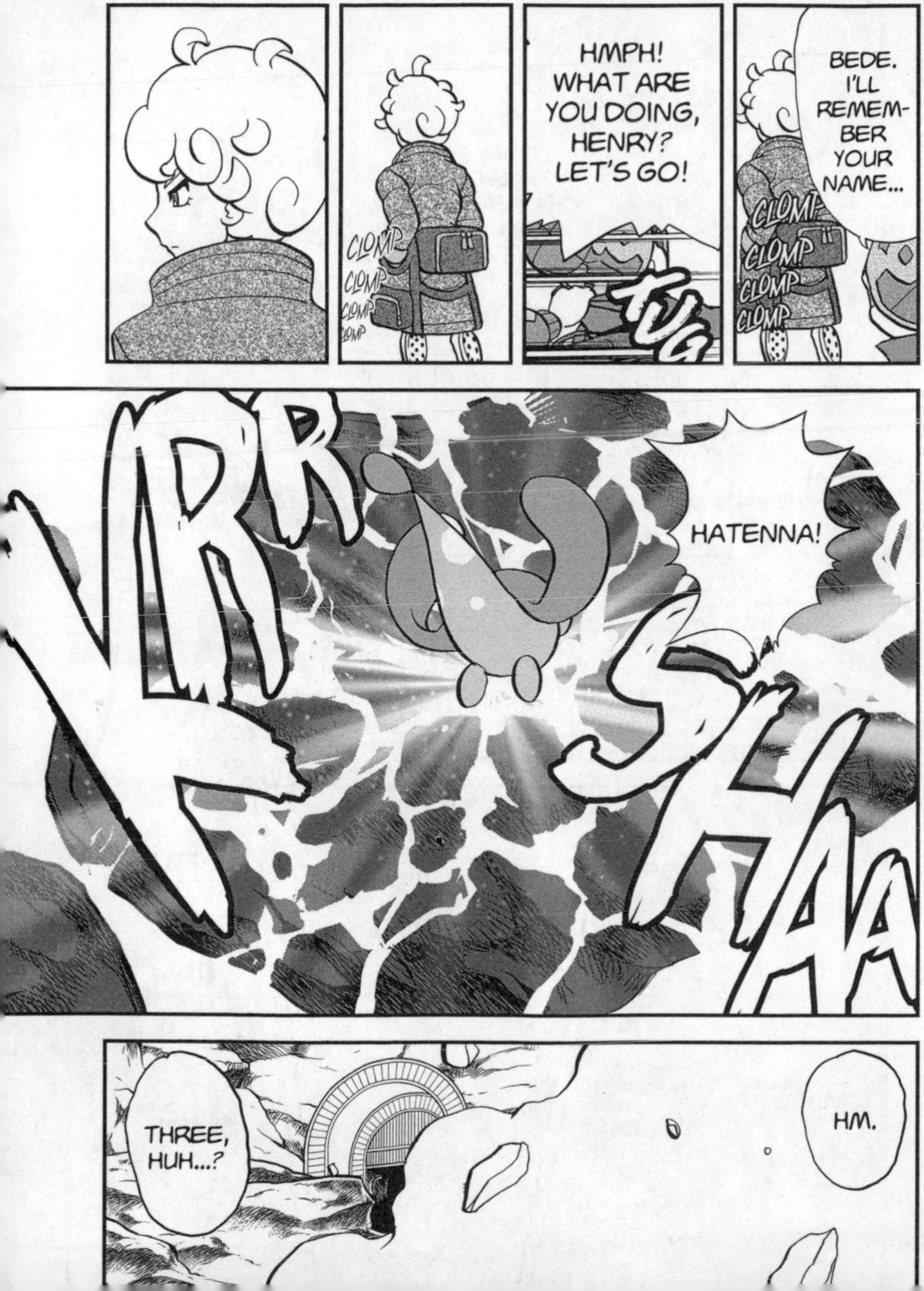
BEDE. I'LL REMEMBER YOUR NAME...
CLOMP CLOMP CLOMP CLOMP
HMPH! WHAT ARE YOU DOING, HENRY? LET'S GO!
TUG
CLOMP CLOMP CLOMP CLOMP
HATENNA!
SHAA
VRR
HM.
THREE, HUH...?

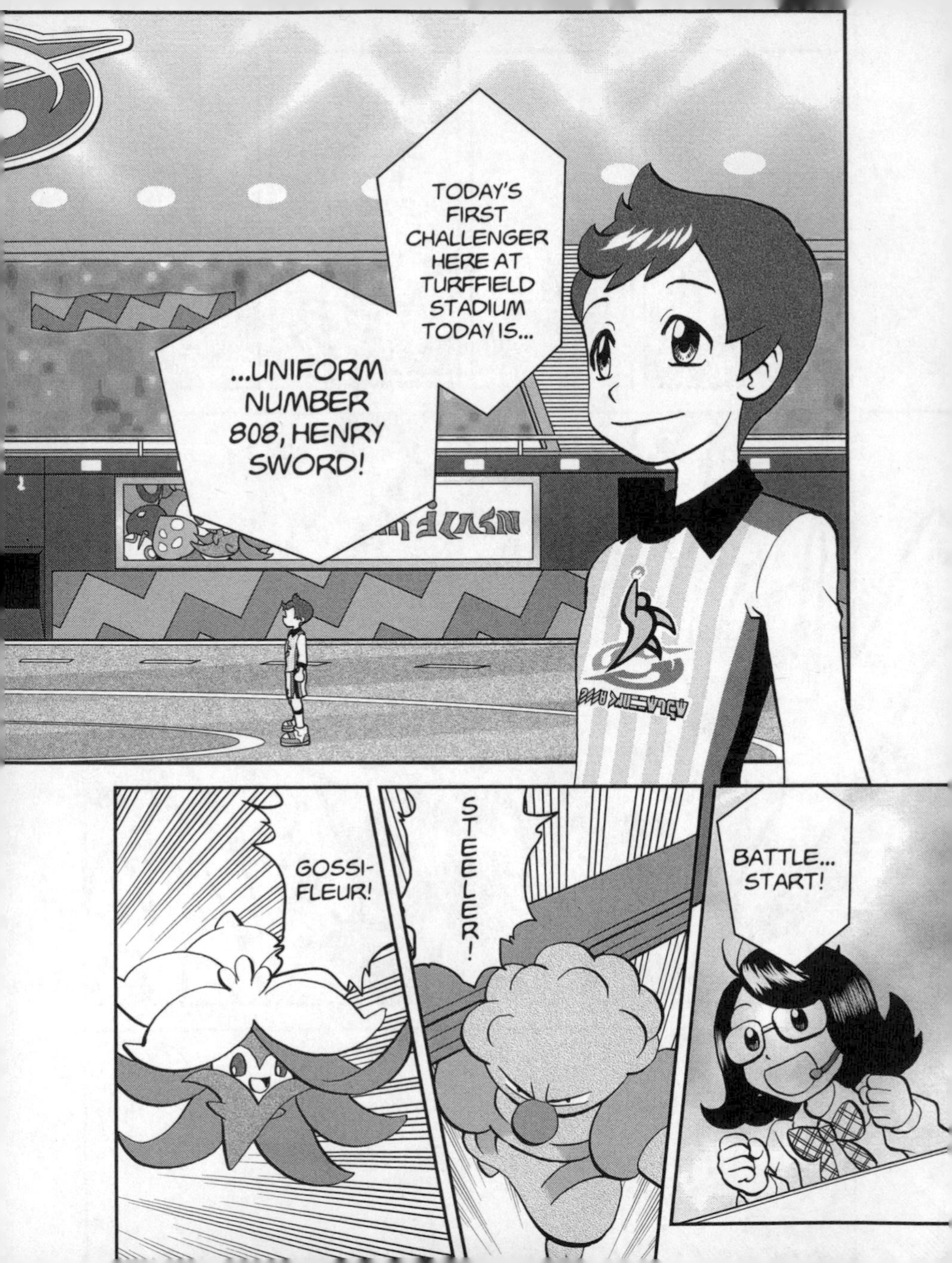
TODAY'S FIRST CHALLENGER HERE AT TURFFIELD STADIUM TODAY IS...
...UNIFORM NUMBER 808, HENRY SWORD!
BATTLE... START!
STEELER!
GOSSI-FLEUR!

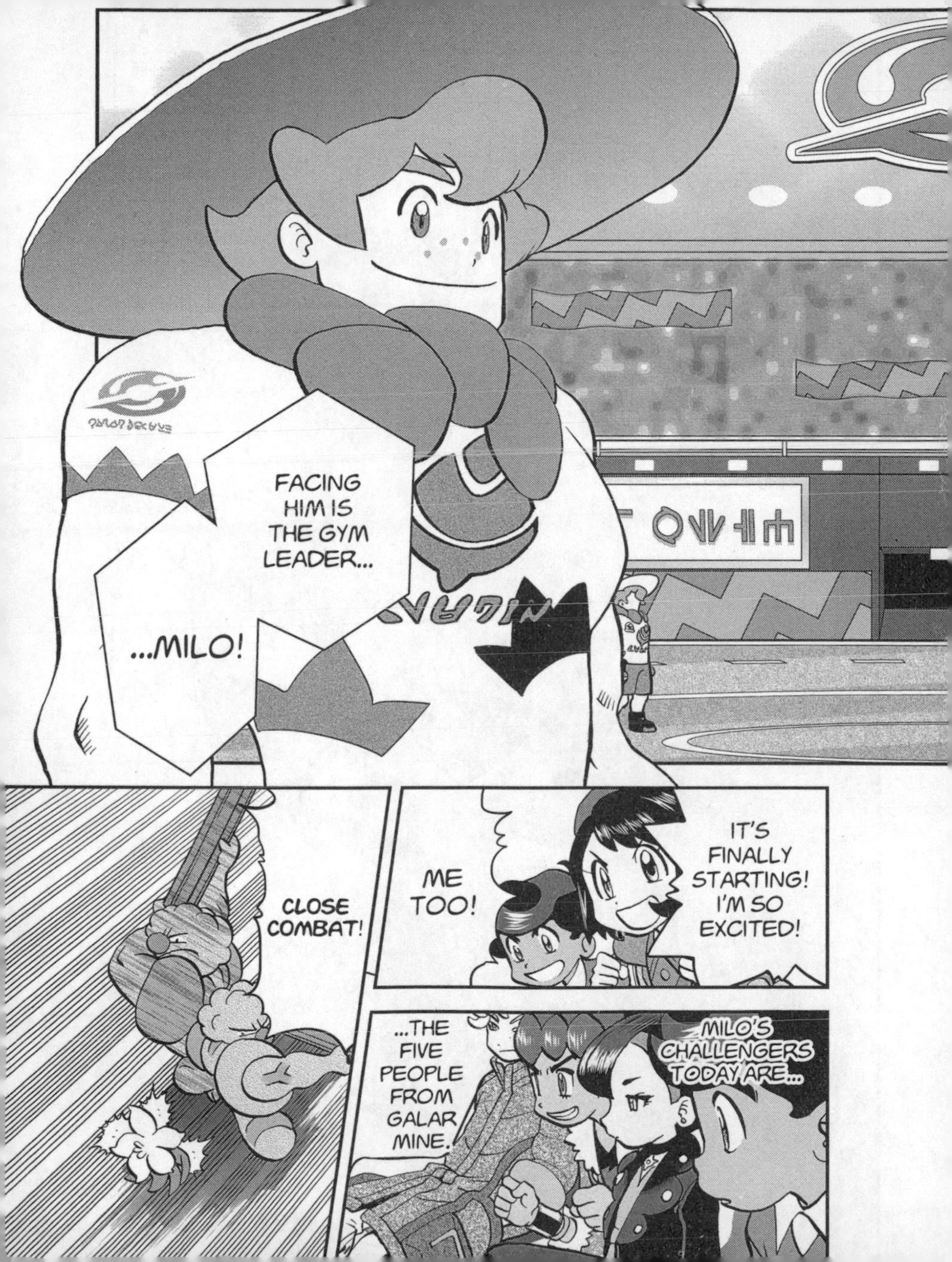
FACING HIM IS THE GYM LEADER...
...MILO!
IT'S FINALLY STARTING! I'M SO EXCITED!
ME TOO!
MILO'S CHALLENGERS TODAY ARE...
...THE FIVE PEOPLE FROM GALAR MINE.
CLOSE COMBAT!

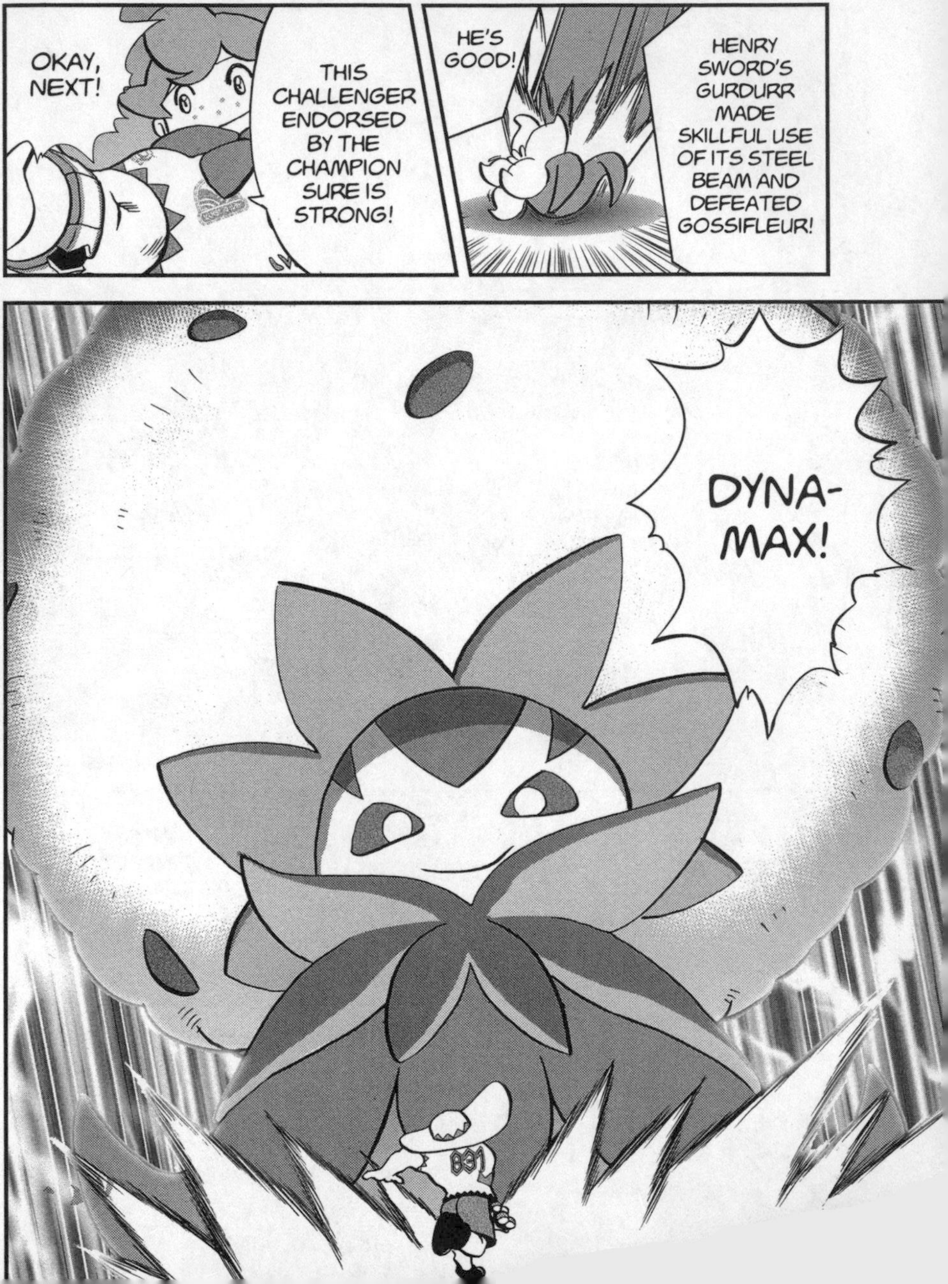
HENRY SWORD'S GURDURR MADE SKILLFUL USE OF ITS STEEL BEAM AND DEFEATED GOSSIFLEUR!
HE'S GOOD!
THIS CHALLENGER ENDORSED BY THE CHAMPION SURE IS STRONG!
OKAY, NEXT!
DYNA-MAX!

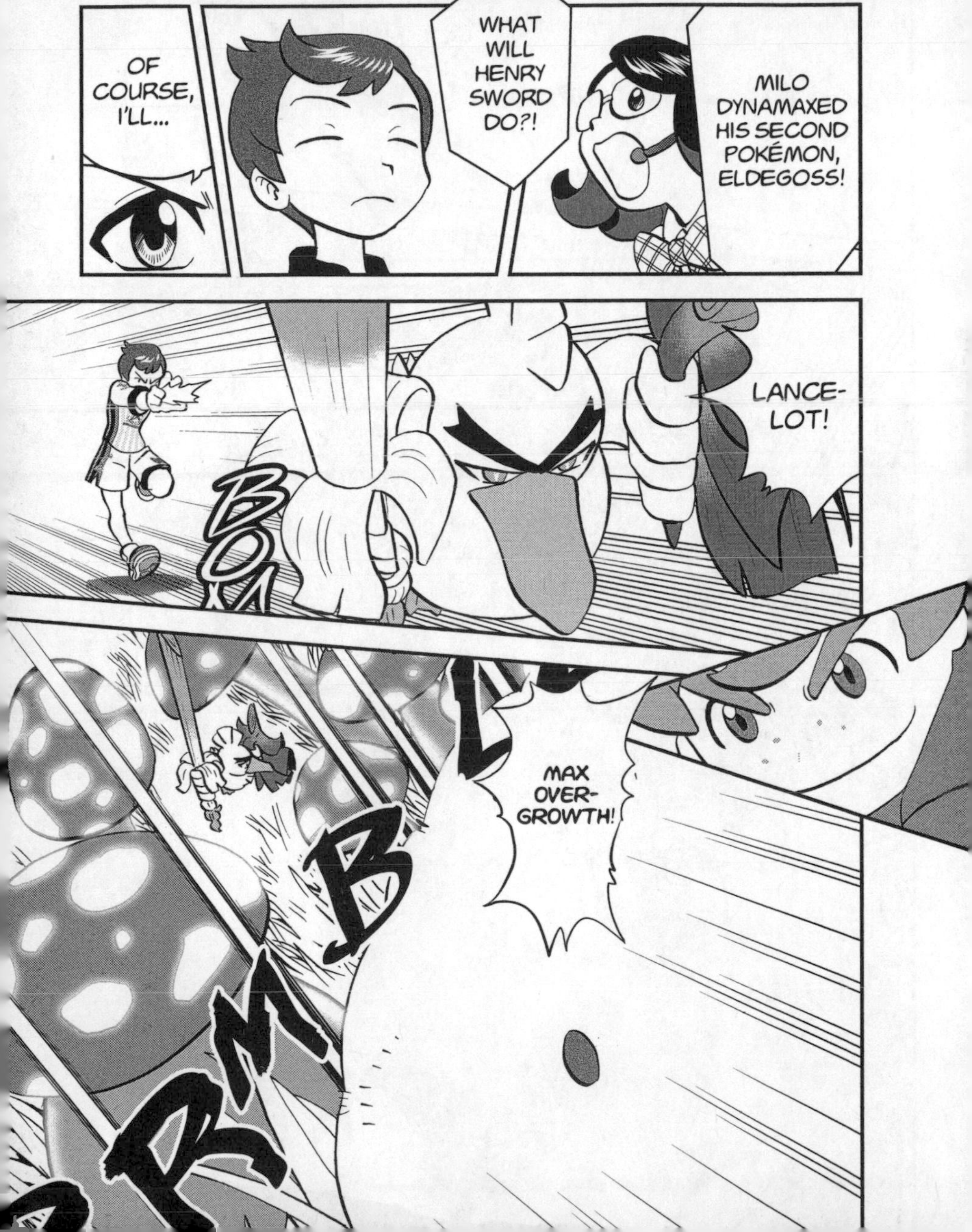
MILO DYNAMAXED HIS SECOND POKÉMON, ELDEGOSS!
WHAT WILL HENRY SWORD DO?!
OF COURSE, I'LL...
LANCE-LOT!
MAX OVER-GROWTH!

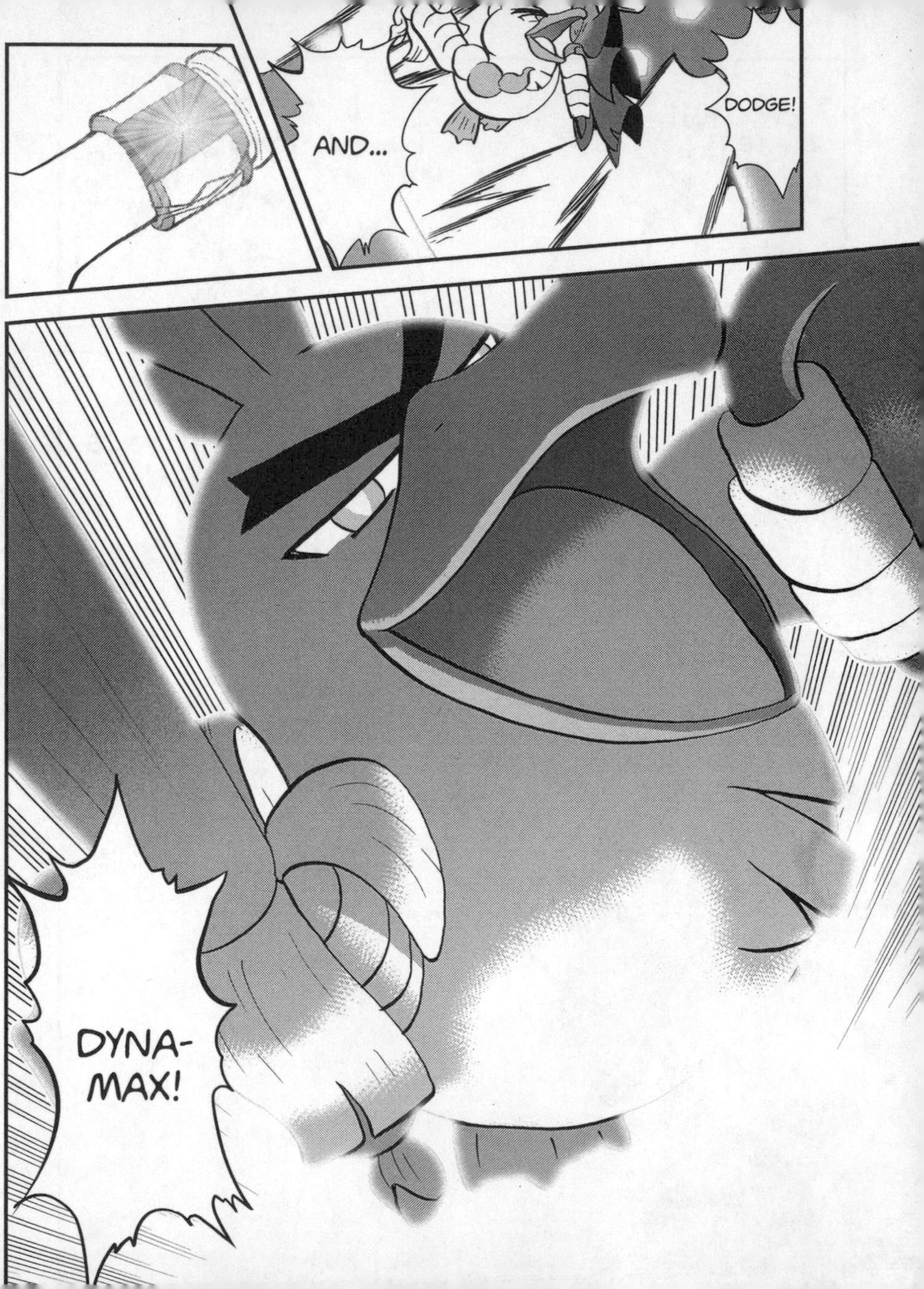
DODGE!
AND...
DYNA-MAX!

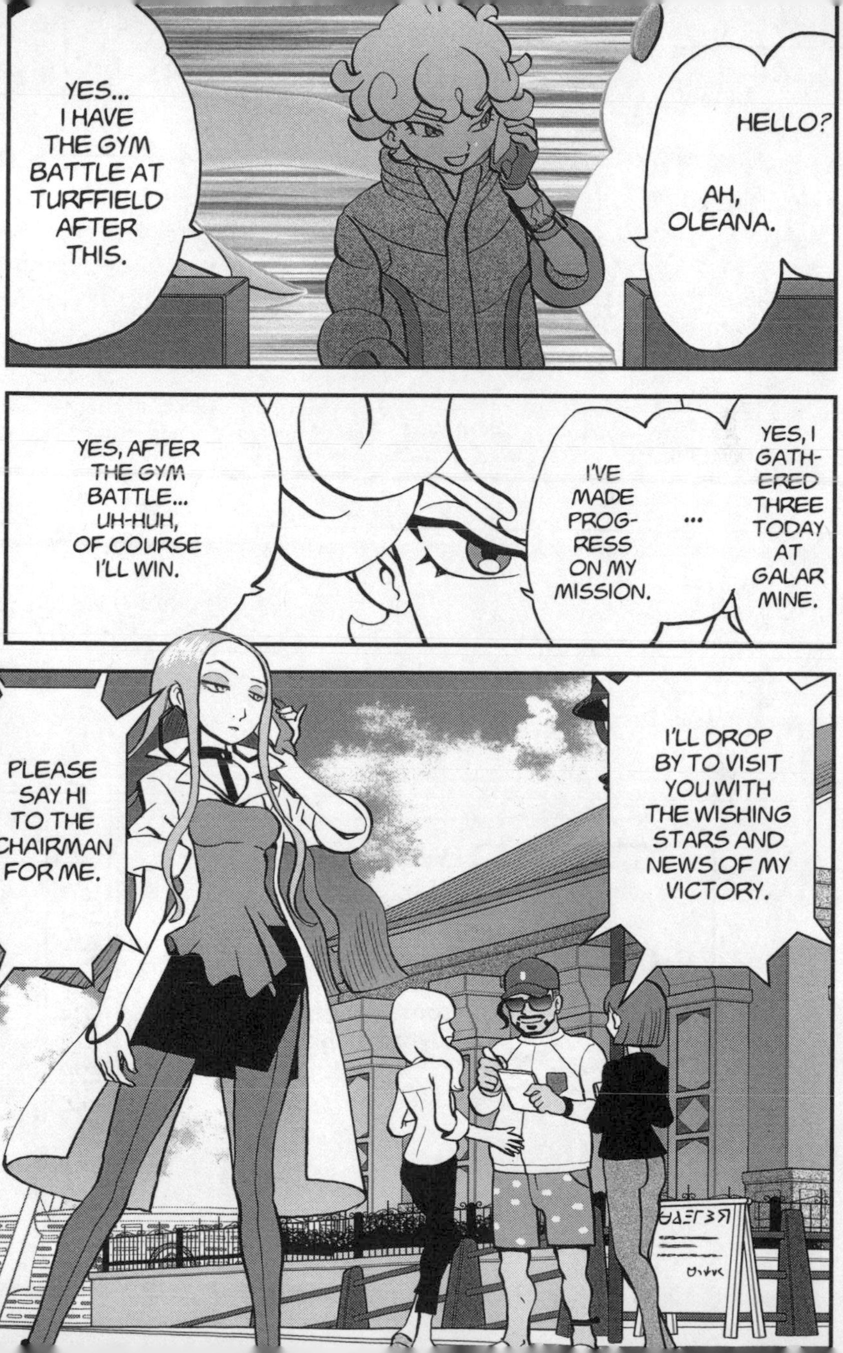
HELLO?
AH, OLEANA.
YES... I HAVE THE GYM BATTLE AT TURFFIELD AFTER THIS.
YES, I GATHERED THREE TODAY AT GALAR MINE.
...
I'VE MADE PROGRESS ON MY MISSION.
YES, AFTER THE GYM BATTLE... UH-HUH, OF COURSE I'LL WIN.
I'LL DROP BY TO VISIT YOU WITH THE WISHING STARS AND NEWS OF MY VICTORY.
PLEASE SAY HI TO THE CHAIRMAN FOR ME.

THE SECRETS OF DYNAMAX, PART 6

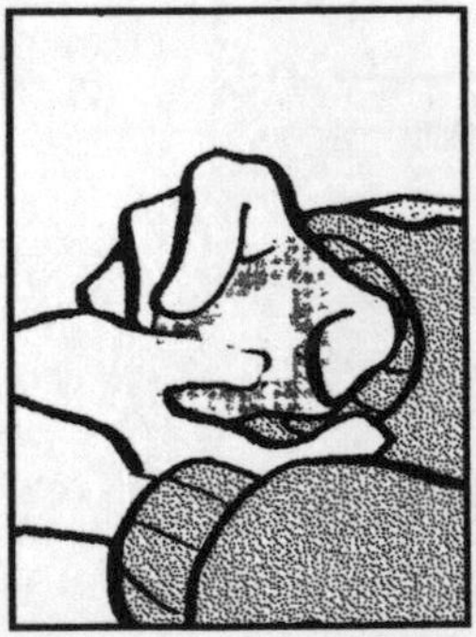

▲They say your wish will come true if you find one!

Wishing Star

Professor Magnolia is currently researching these stones found in the Galar region. They have some connection to the Dynamax phenomenon...

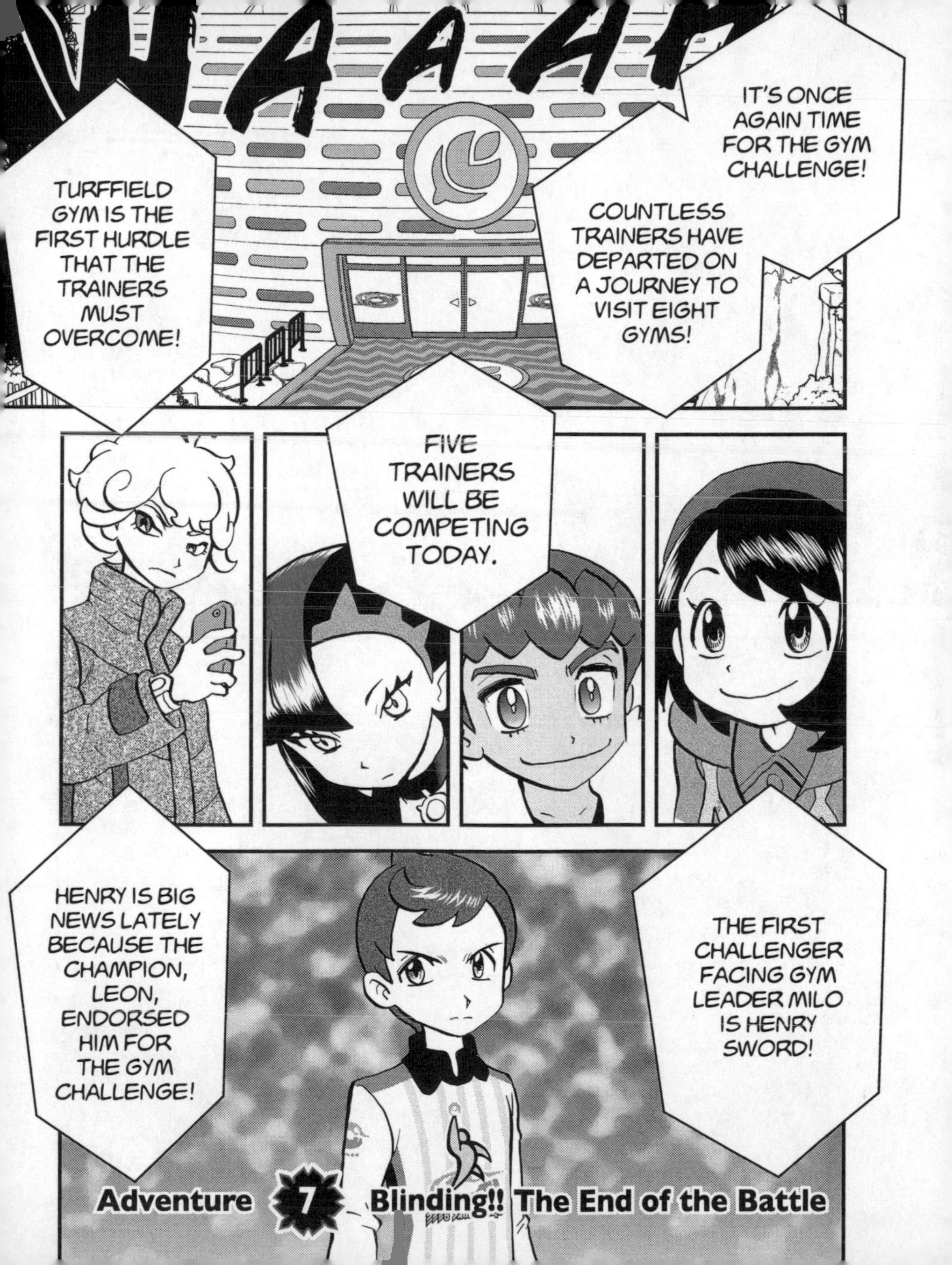
IT'S ONCE AGAIN TIME FOR THE GYM CHALLENGE!
COUNTLESS TRAINERS HAVE DEPARTED ON A JOURNEY TO VISIT EIGHT GYMS!
TURFFIELD GYM IS THE FIRST HURDLE THAT THE TRAINERS MUST OVERCOME!
FIVE TRAINERS WILL BE COMPETING TODAY.
THE FIRST CHALLENGER FACING GYM LEADER MILO IS HENRY SWORD!
HENRY IS BIG NEWS LATELY BECAUSE THE CHAMPION, LEON, ENDORSED HIM FOR THE GYM CHALLENGE!

Adventure 7 Blinding!! The End of the Battle

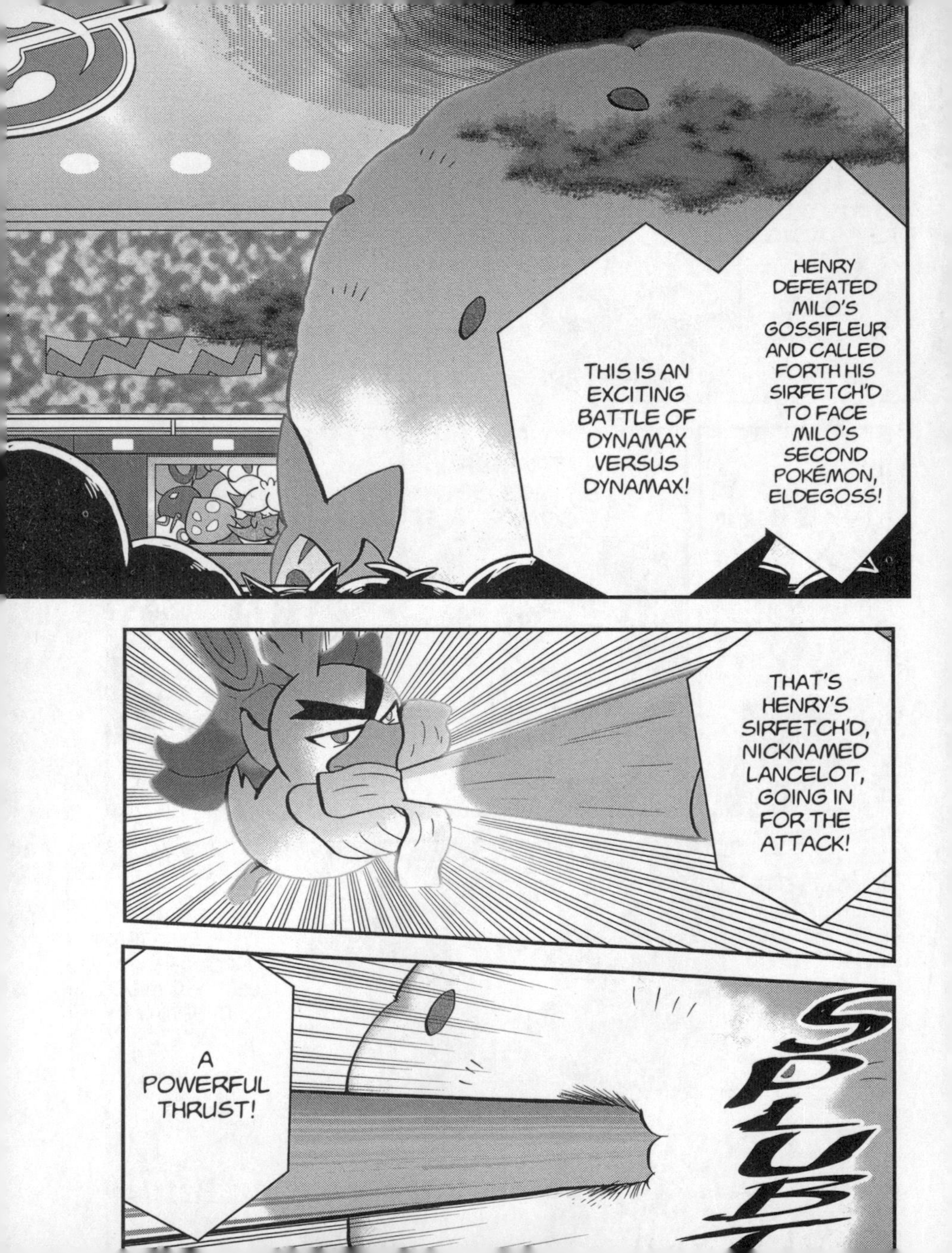
HENRY DEFEATED MILO'S GOSSIFLEUR AND CALLED FORTH HIS SIRFETCH'D TO FACE MILO'S SECOND POKÉMON, ELDEGOSS!
THIS IS AN EXCITING BATTLE OF DYNAMAX VERSUS DYNAMAX!
THAT'S HENRY'S SIRFETCH'D, NICKNAMED LANCELOT, GOING IN FOR THE ATTACK!
SPLUB
A POWERFUL THRUST!

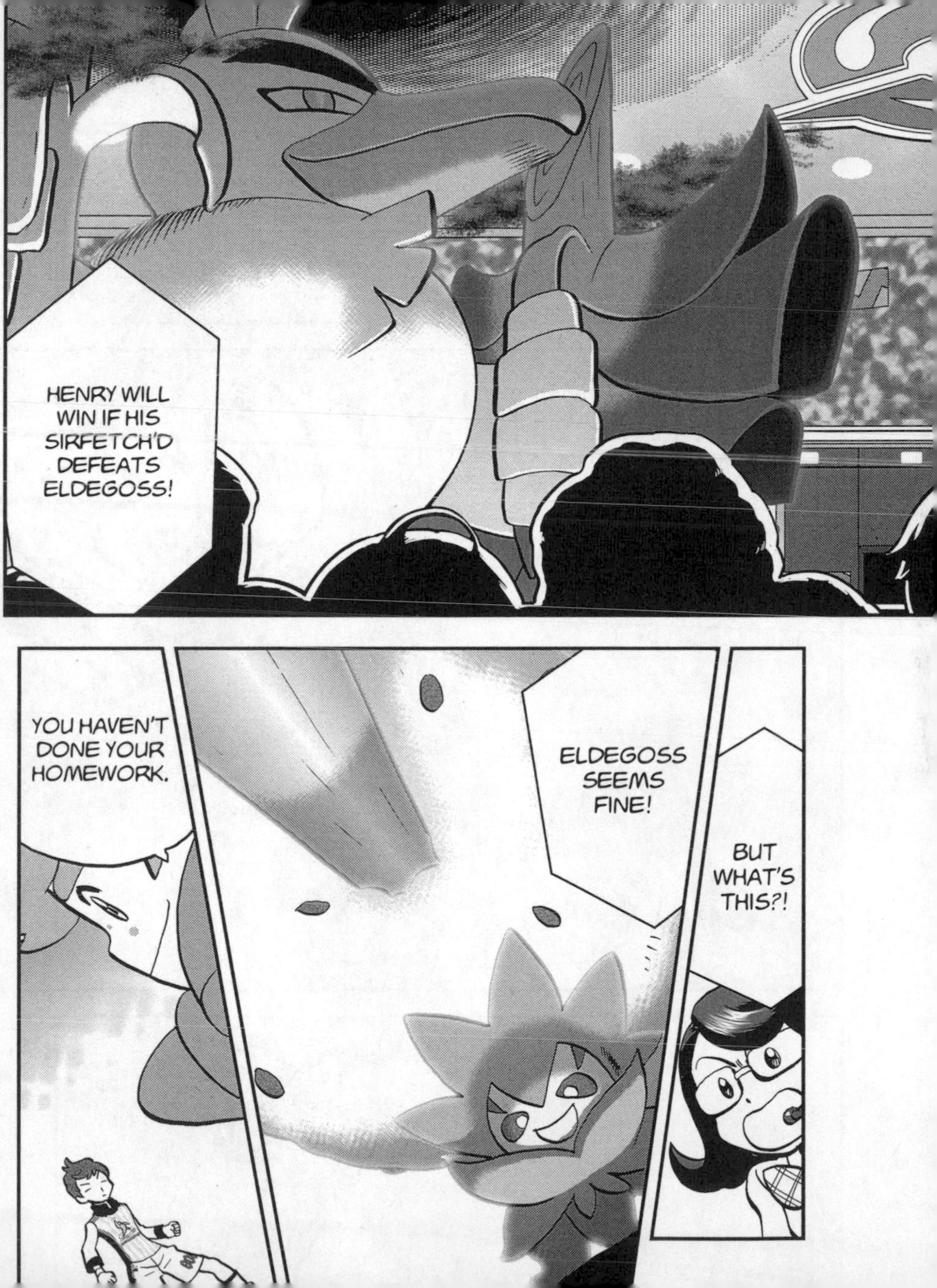
HENRY WILL WIN IF HIS SIRFETCH'D DEFEATS ELDEGOSS!
ELDEGOSS SEEMS FINE!
BUT WHAT'S THIS?!
YOU HAVEN'T DONE YOUR HOMEWORK.

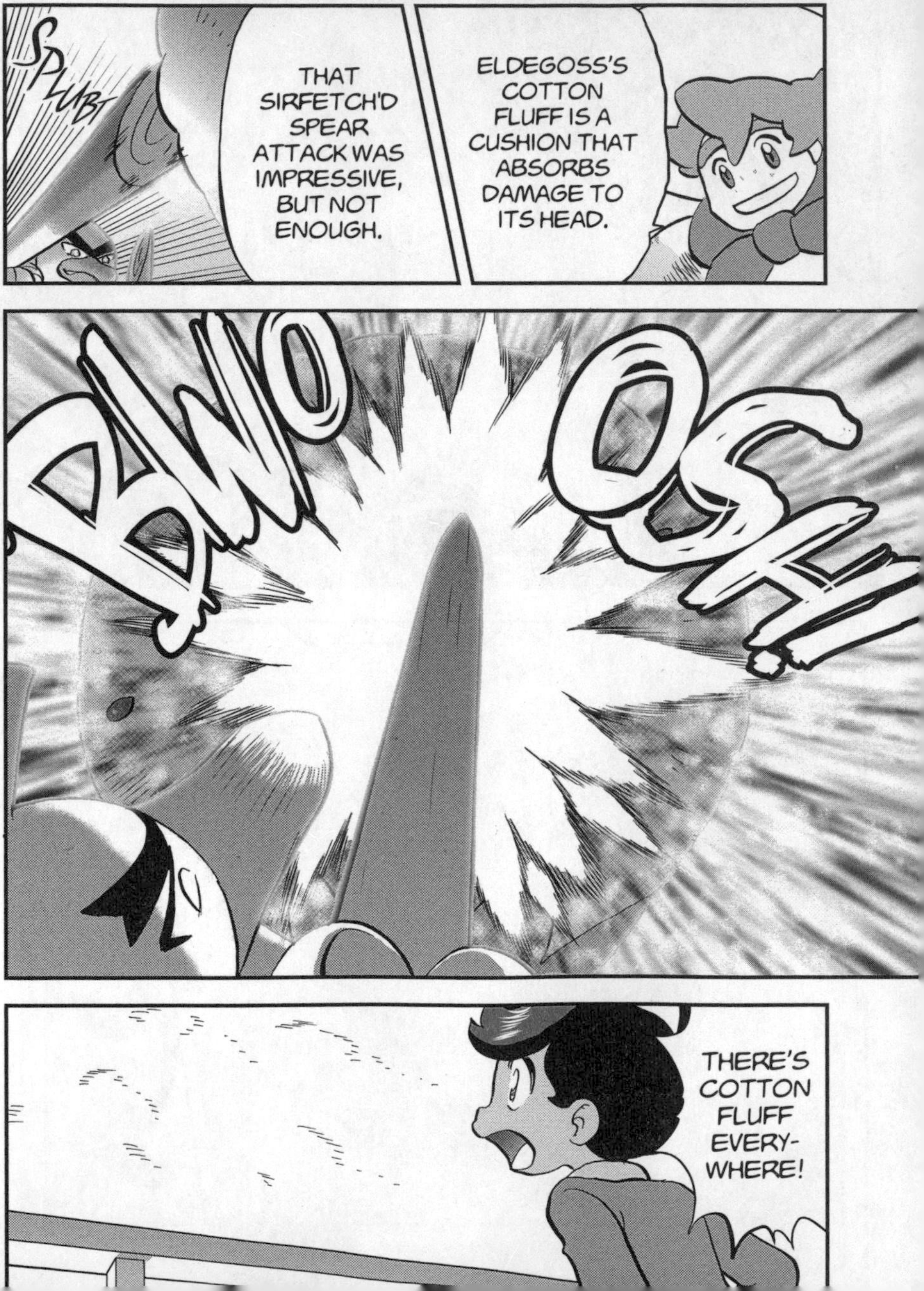
ELDEGOSS'S COTTON FLUFF IS A CUSHION THAT ABSORBS DAMAGE TO ITS HEAD.
THAT SIRFETCH'D SPEAR ATTACK WAS IMPRESSIVE, BUT NOT ENOUGH.
SPLUBT
BWOOSH!!
THERE'S COTTON FLUFF EVERY-WHERE!

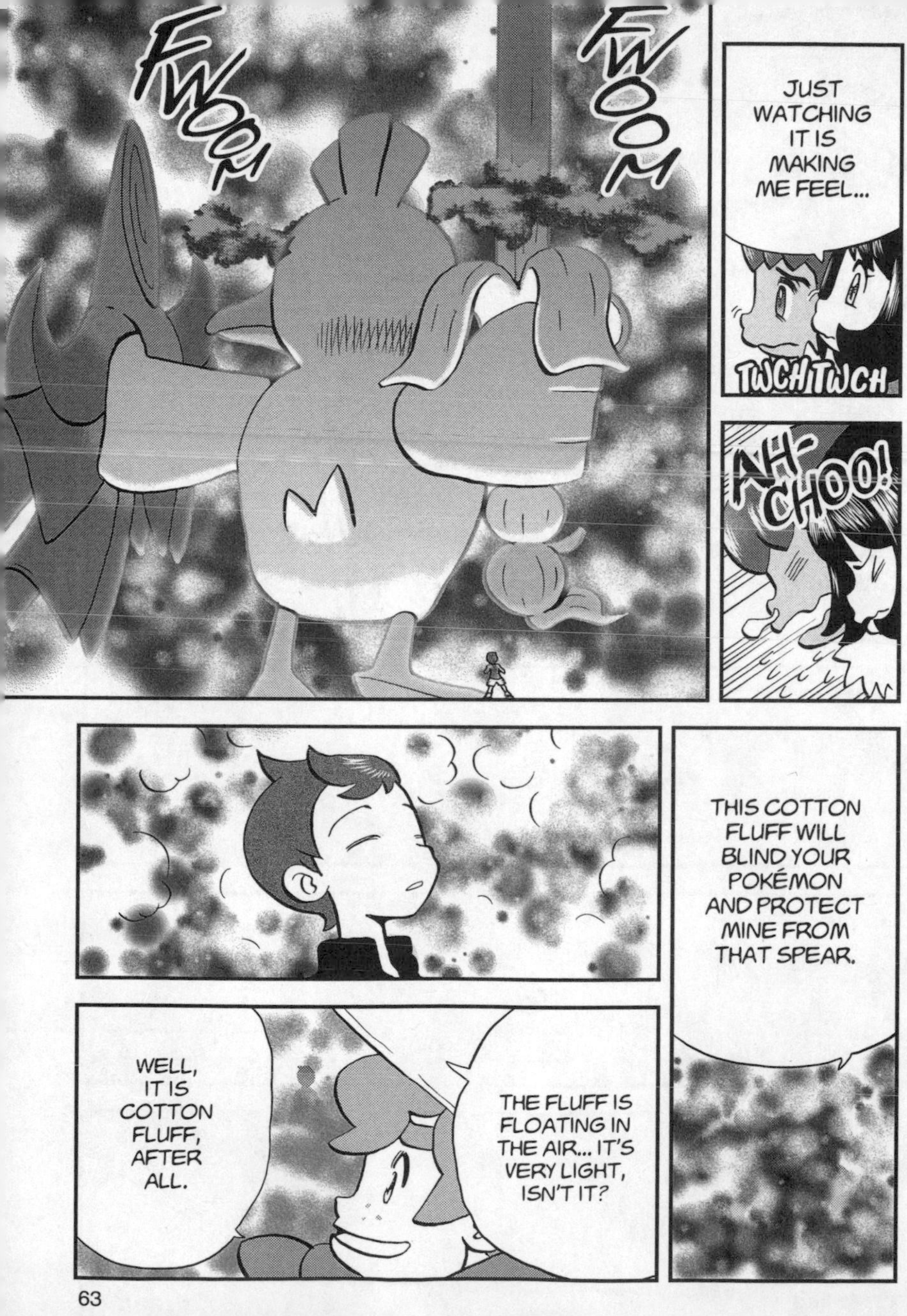
JUST WATCHING IT IS MAKING ME FEEL...
TWCH TWCH
AH-CHOO!
FWOOM
FWOOM
THIS COTTON FLUFF WILL BLIND YOUR POKÉMON AND PROTECT MINE FROM THAT SPEAR.
THE FLUFF IS FLOATING IN THE AIR... IT'S VERY LIGHT, ISN'T IT?
WELL, IT IS COTTON FLUFF, AFTER ALL.

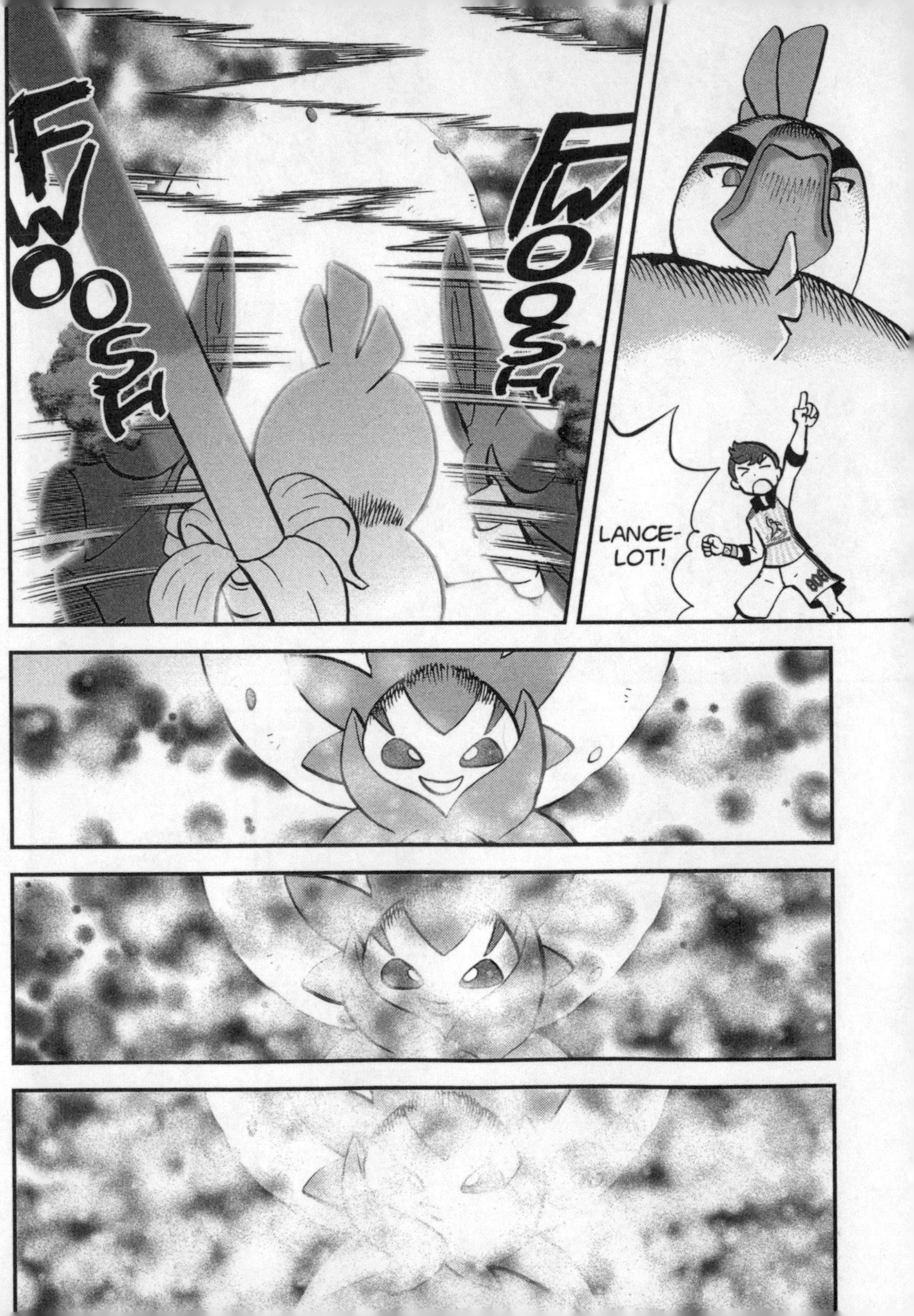
LANCE-LOT!
FWOOSH
FWOOSH

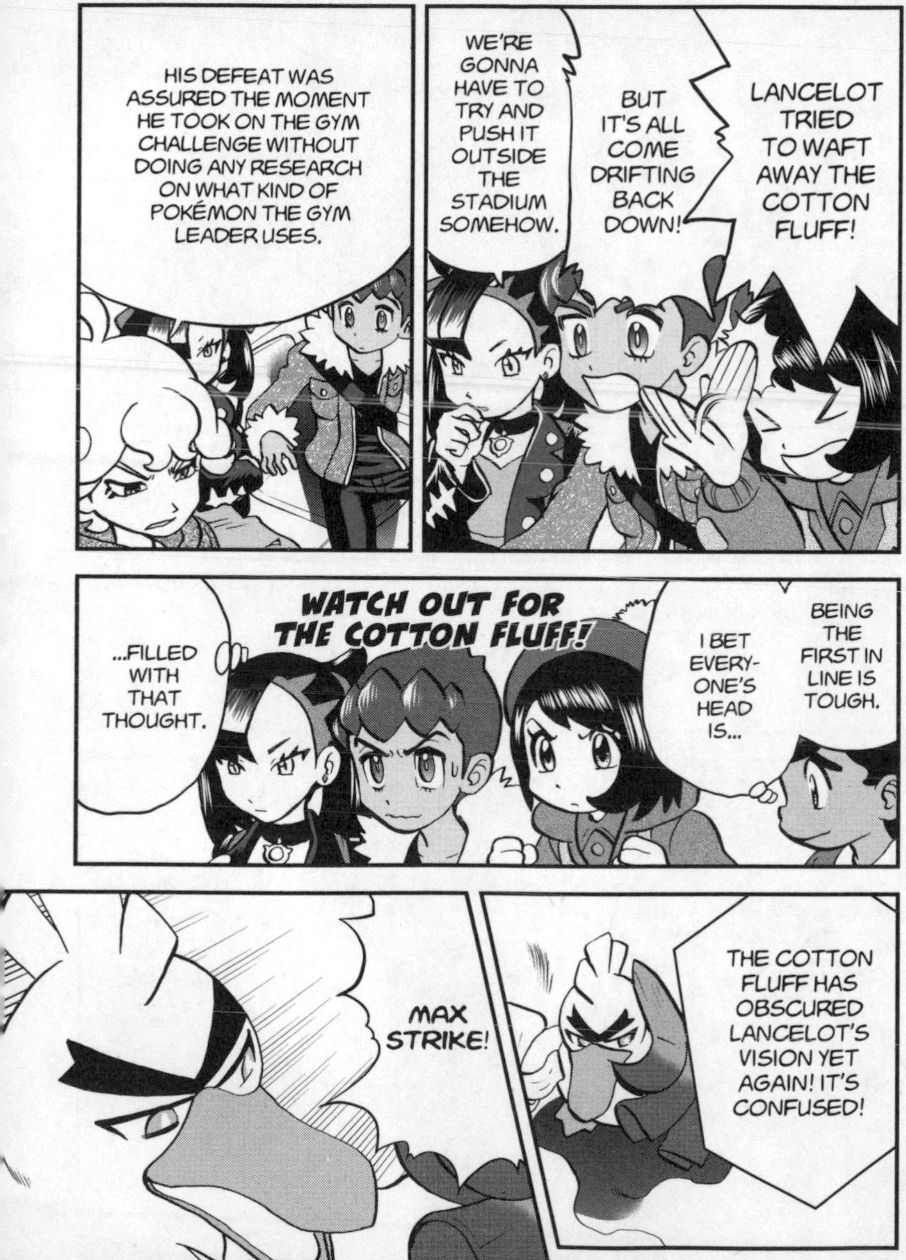
LANCELOT TRIED TO WAFT AWAY THE COTTON FLUFF!
BUT IT'S ALL COME DRIFTING BACK DOWN!
WE'RE GONNA HAVE TO TRY AND PUSH IT OUTSIDE THE STADIUM SOMEHOW.
HIS DEFEAT WAS ASSURED THE MOMENT HE TOOK ON THE GYM CHALLENGE WITHOUT DOING ANY RESEARCH ON WHAT KIND OF POKÉMON THE GYM LEADER USES.
BEING THE FIRST IN LINE IS TOUGH.
I BET EVERY-ONE'S HEAD IS...
WATCH OUT FOR THE COTTON FLUFF!
...FILLED WITH THAT THOUGHT.
THE COTTON FLUFF HAS OBSCURED LANCELOT'S VISION YET AGAIN! IT'S CONFUSED!
MAX STRIKE!

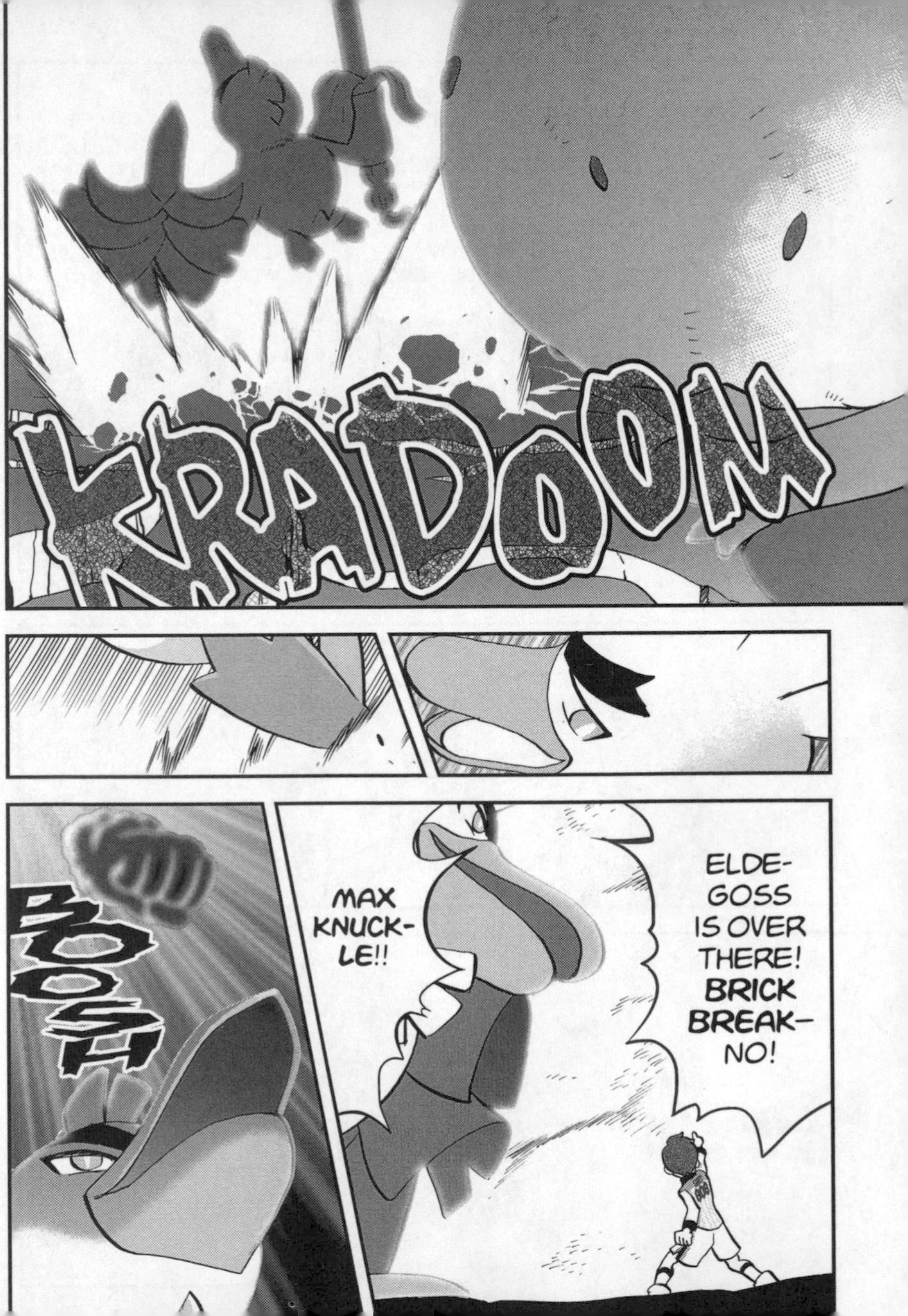
KRADOOM
ELDE-GOSS IS OVER THERE! BRICK BREAK— NO!
MAX KNUCK-LE!!
BOOSH

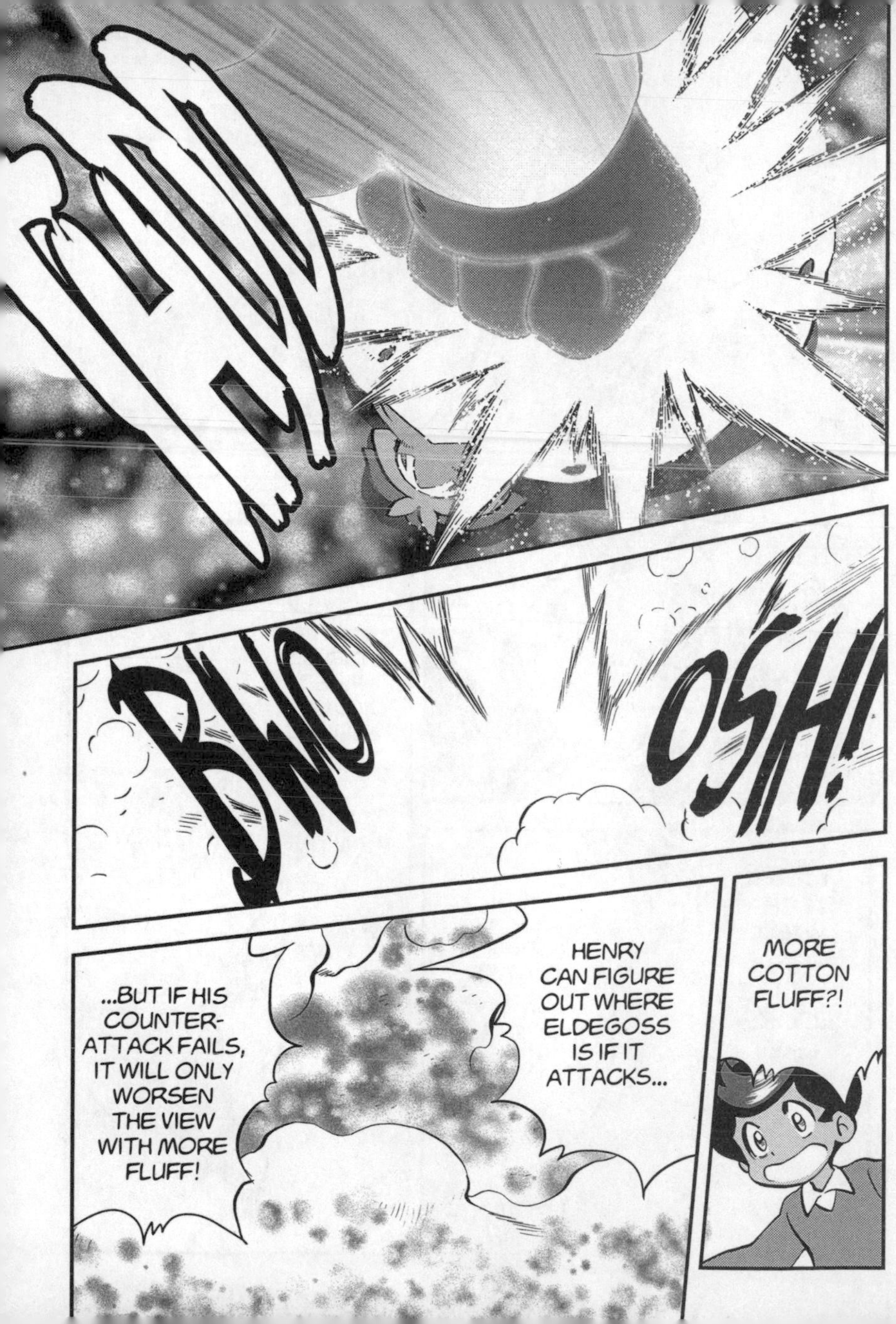
BWOOSH!
MORE COTTON FLUFF?!
HENRY CAN FIGURE OUT WHERE ELDEGOSS IS IF IT ATTACKS...
...BUT IF HIS COUNTER-ATTACK FAILS, IT WILL ONLY WORSEN THE VIEW WITH MORE FLUFF!

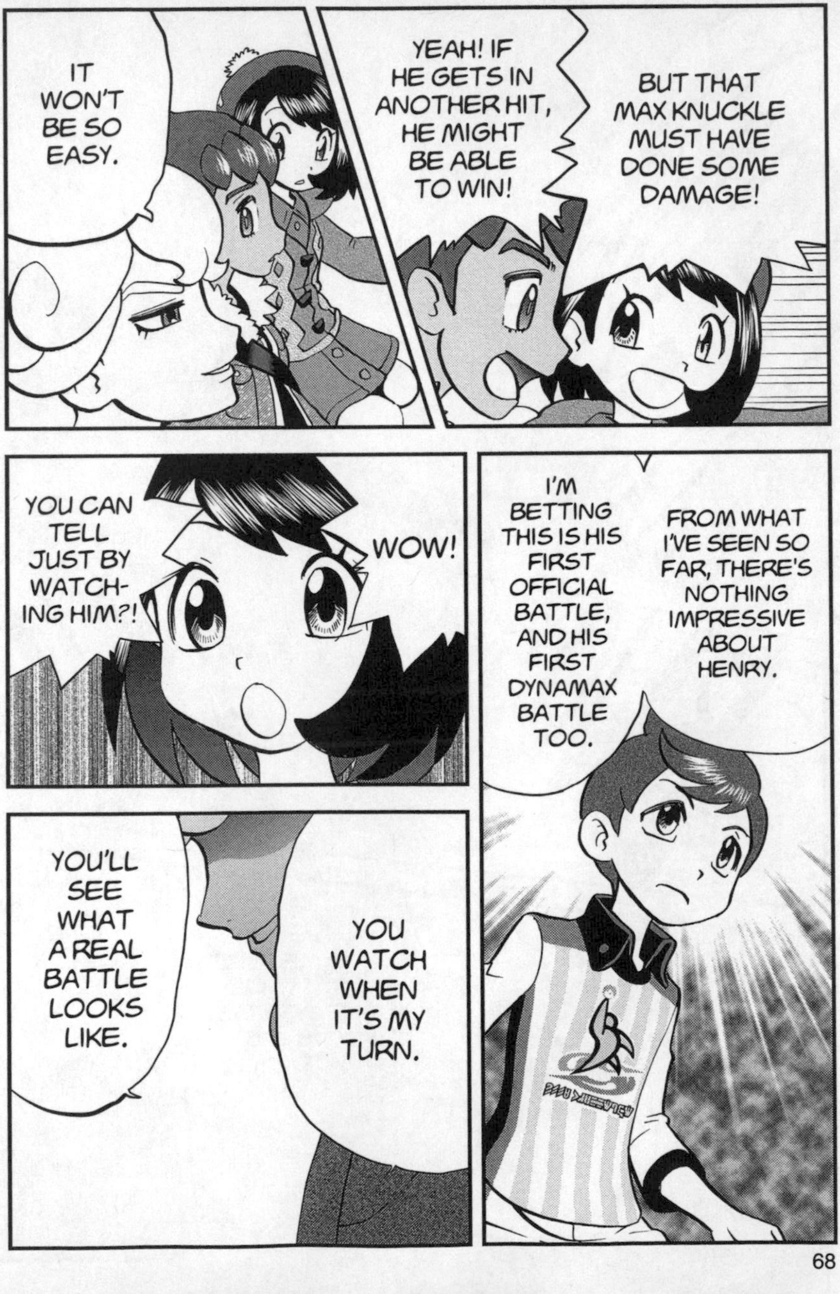
BUT THAT MAX KNUCKLE MUST HAVE DONE SOME DAMAGE!
YEAH! IF HE GETS IN ANOTHER HIT, HE MIGHT BE ABLE TO WIN!
IT WON'T BE SO EASY.
FROM WHAT I'VE SEEN SO FAR, THERE'S NOTHING IMPRESSIVE ABOUT HENRY.
I'M BETTING THIS IS HIS FIRST OFFICIAL BATTLE, AND HIS FIRST DYNAMAX BATTLE TOO.
WOW!
YOU CAN TELL JUST BY WATCHING HIM?!
YOU WATCH WHEN IT'S MY TURN.
YOU'LL SEE WHAT A REAL BATTLE LOOKS LIKE.

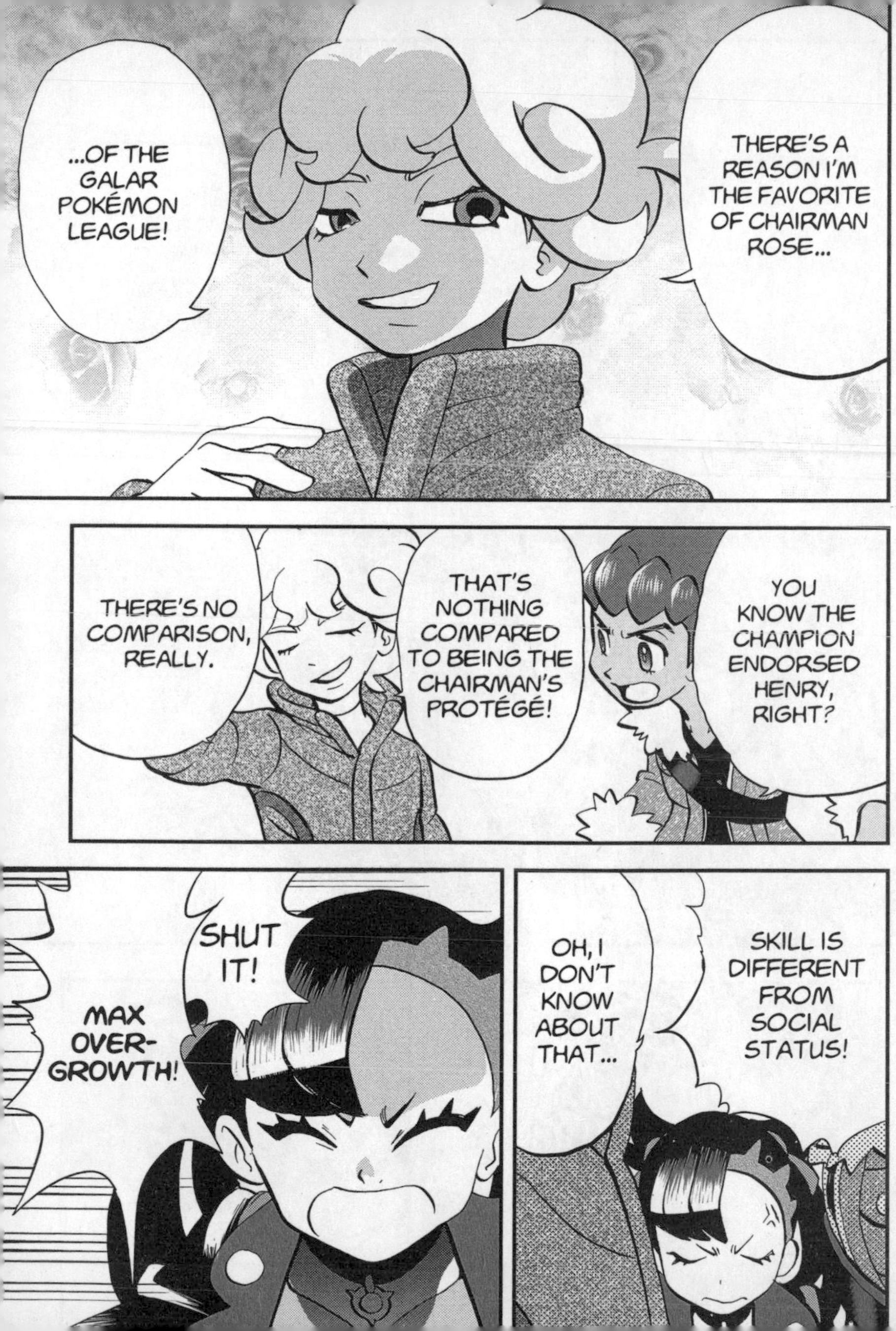
THERE'S A REASON I'M THE FAVORITE OF CHAIRMAN ROSE...
...OF THE GALAR POKÉMON LEAGUE!
YOU KNOW THE CHAMPION ENDORSED HENRY, RIGHT?
THAT'S NOTHING COMPARED TO BEING THE CHAIRMAN'S PROTÉGÉ!
THERE'S NO COMPARISON, REALLY.
SKILL IS DIFFERENT FROM SOCIAL STATUS!
OH, I DON'T KNOW ABOUT THAT...
SHUT IT!
MAX OVER-GROWTH!

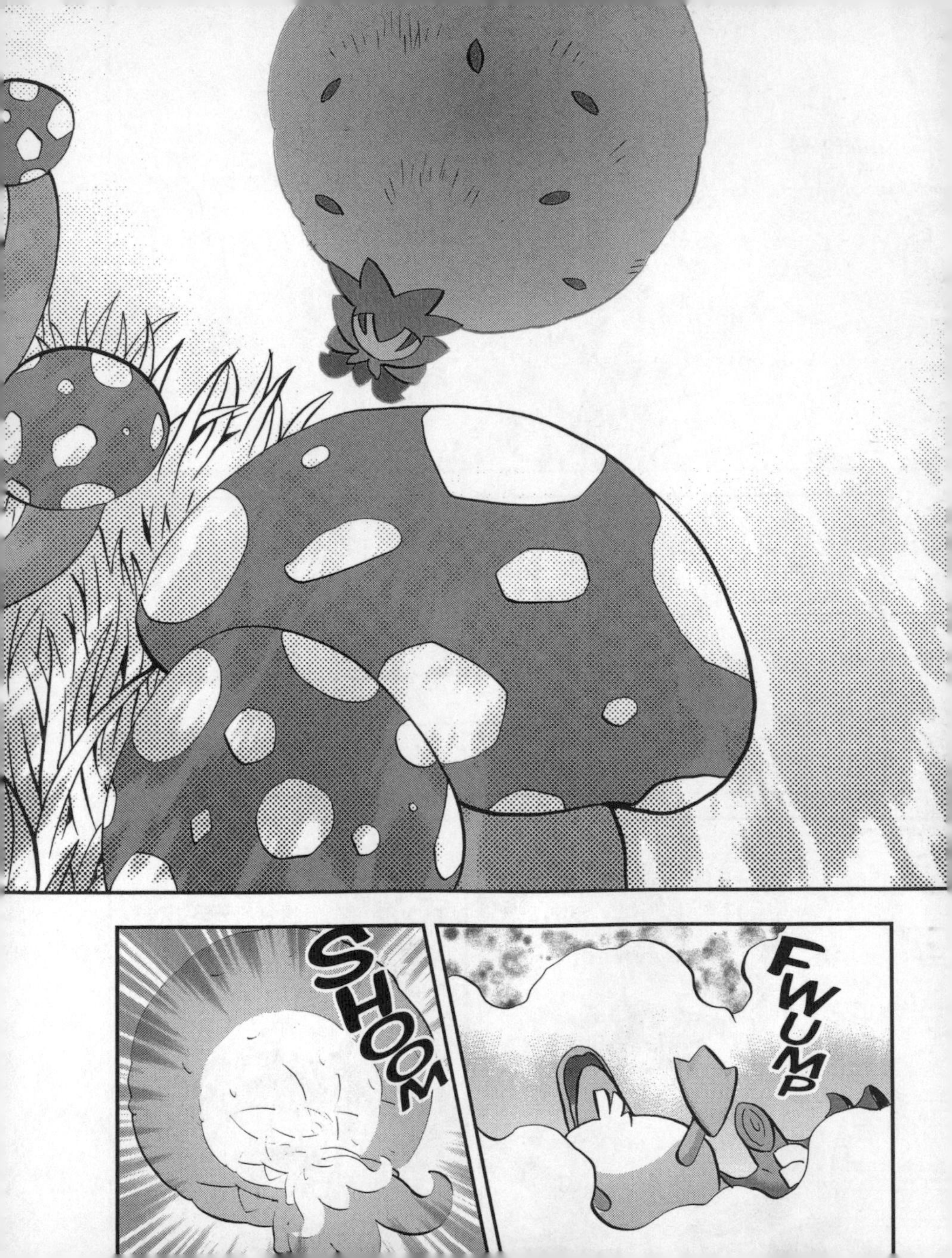
FWUMP
SHOOM

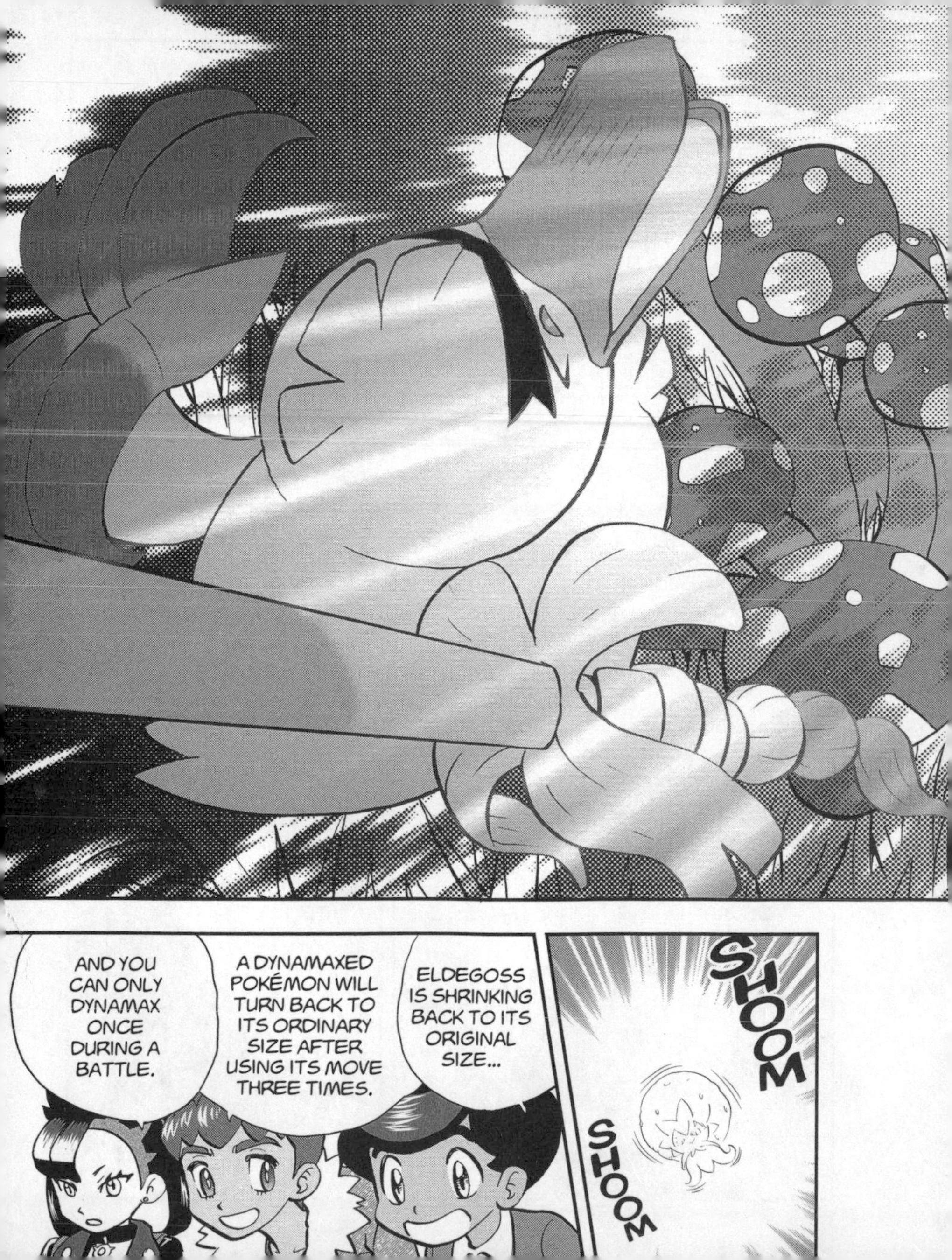
SHOOM
SHOOM
ELDEGOSS IS SHRINKING BACK TO ITS ORIGINAL SIZE...
A DYNAMAXED POKÉMON WILL TURN BACK TO ITS ORDINARY SIZE AFTER USING ITS MOVE THREE TIMES.
AND YOU CAN ONLY DYNAMAX ONCE DURING A BATTLE.

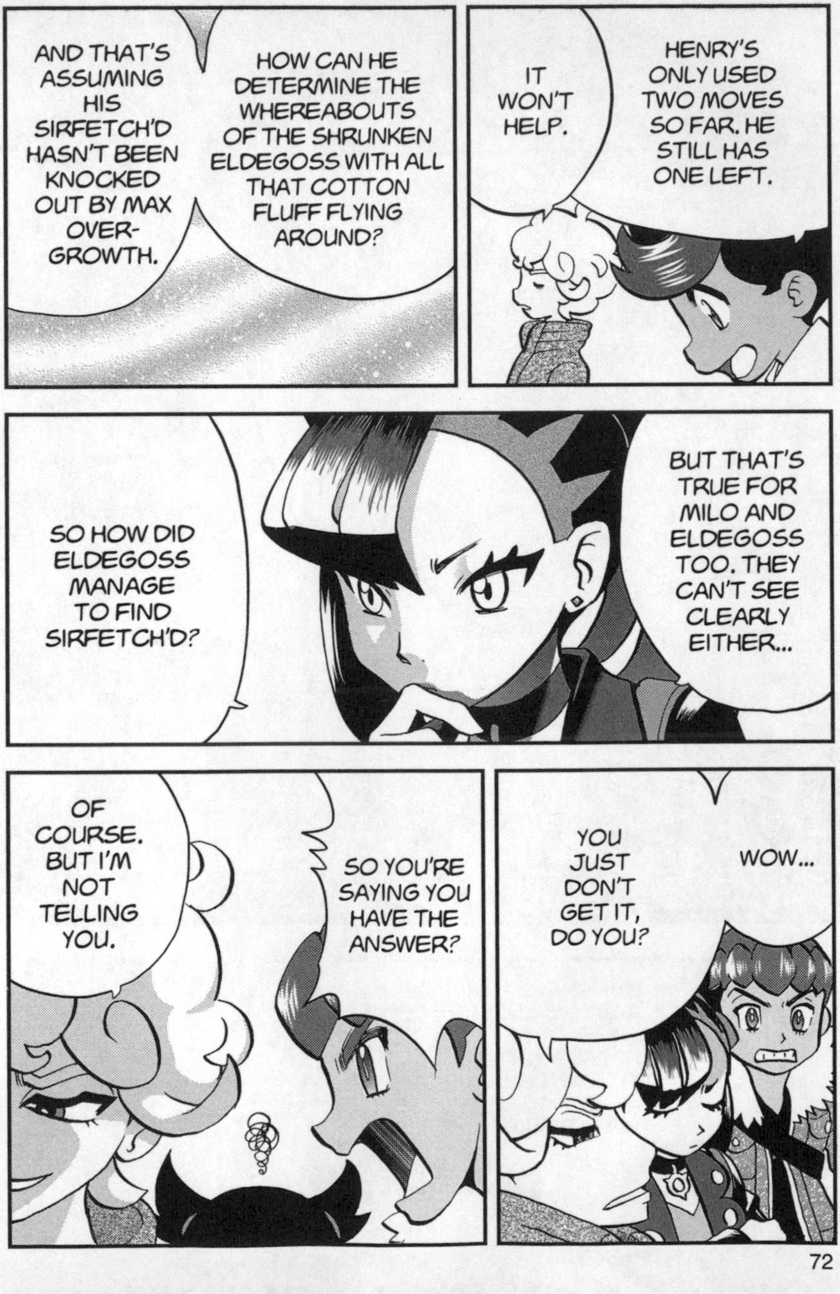
HENRY'S ONLY USED TWO MOVES SO FAR. HE STILL HAS ONE LEFT.
IT WON'T HELP.
HOW CAN HE DETERMINE THE WHEREABOUTS OF THE SHRUNKEN ELDEGOSS WITH ALL THAT COTTON FLUFF FLYING AROUND?
AND THAT'S ASSUMING HIS SIRFETCH'D HASN'T BEEN KNOCKED OUT BY MAX OVER-GROWTH.
BUT THAT'S TRUE FOR MILO AND ELDEGOSS TOO. THEY CAN'T SEE CLEARLY EITHER...
SO HOW DID ELDEGOSS MANAGE TO FIND SIRFETCH'D?
WOW...
YOU JUST DON'T GET IT, DO YOU?
SO YOU'RE SAYING YOU HAVE THE ANSWER?
OF COURSE. BUT I'M NOT TELLING YOU.

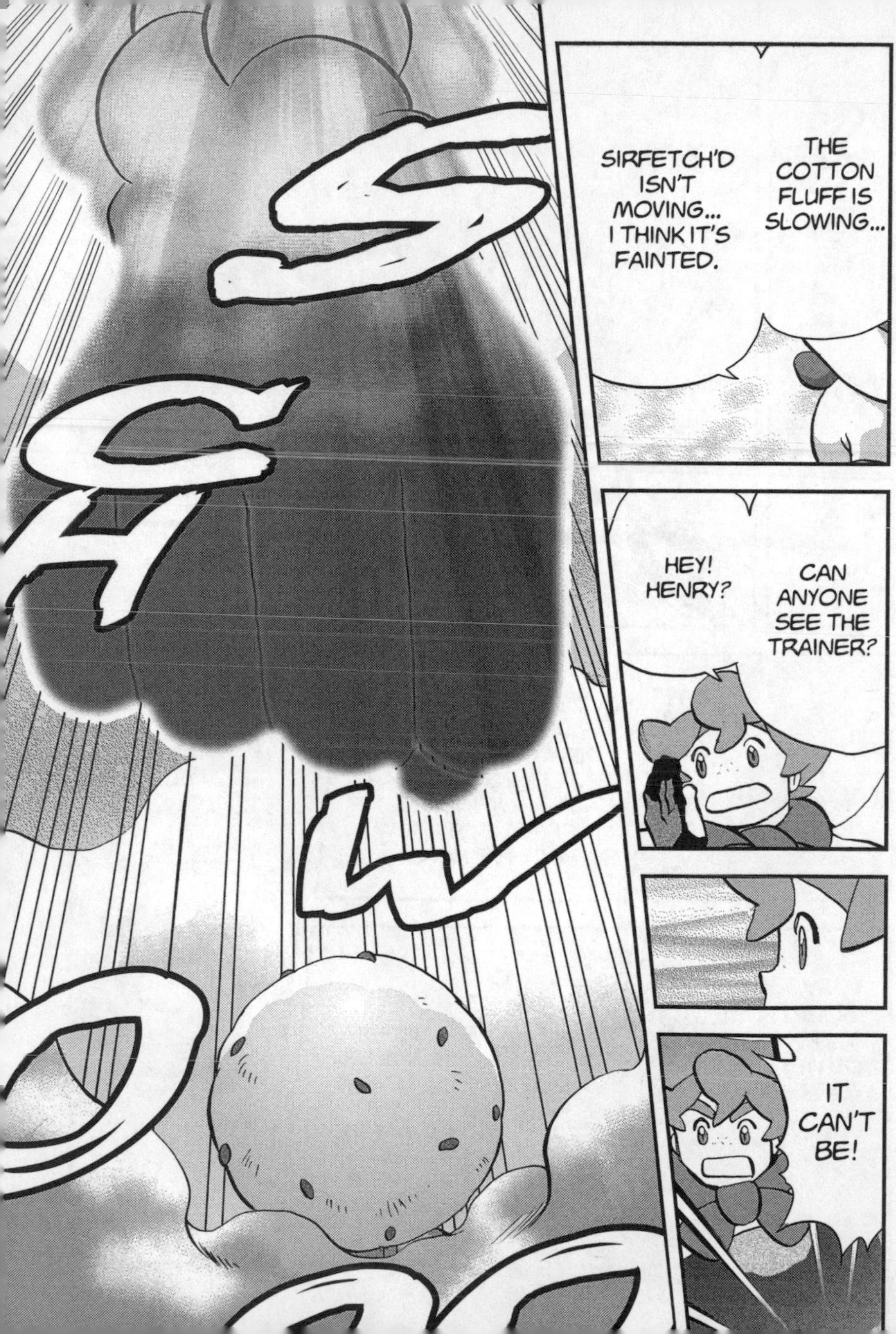
THE COTTON FLUFF IS SLOWING...
SIRFETCH'D ISN'T MOVING... I THINK IT'S FAINTED.
CAN ANYONE SEE THE TRAINER?
HEY! HENRY?
IT CAN'T BE!

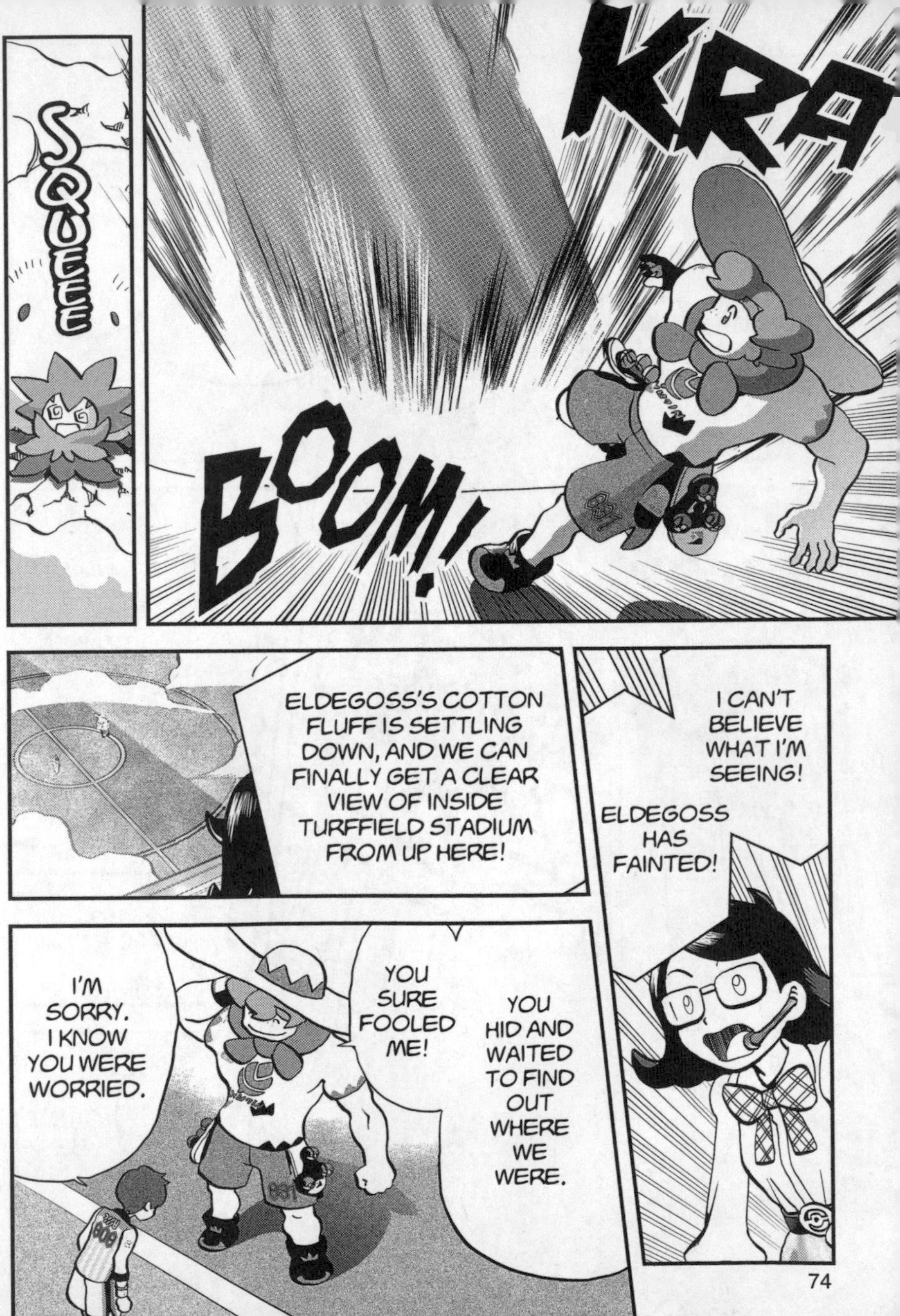
KRA
BOOM!
SQUEEE
I CAN'T BELIEVE WHAT I'M SEEING!
ELDEGOSS HAS FAINTED!
ELDEGOSS'S COTTON FLUFF IS SETTLING DOWN, AND WE CAN FINALLY GET A CLEAR VIEW OF INSIDE TURFFIELD STADIUM FROM UP HERE!
YOU HID AND WAITED TO FIND OUT WHERE WE WERE.
YOU SURE FOOLED ME!
I'M SORRY. I KNOW YOU WERE WORRIED.

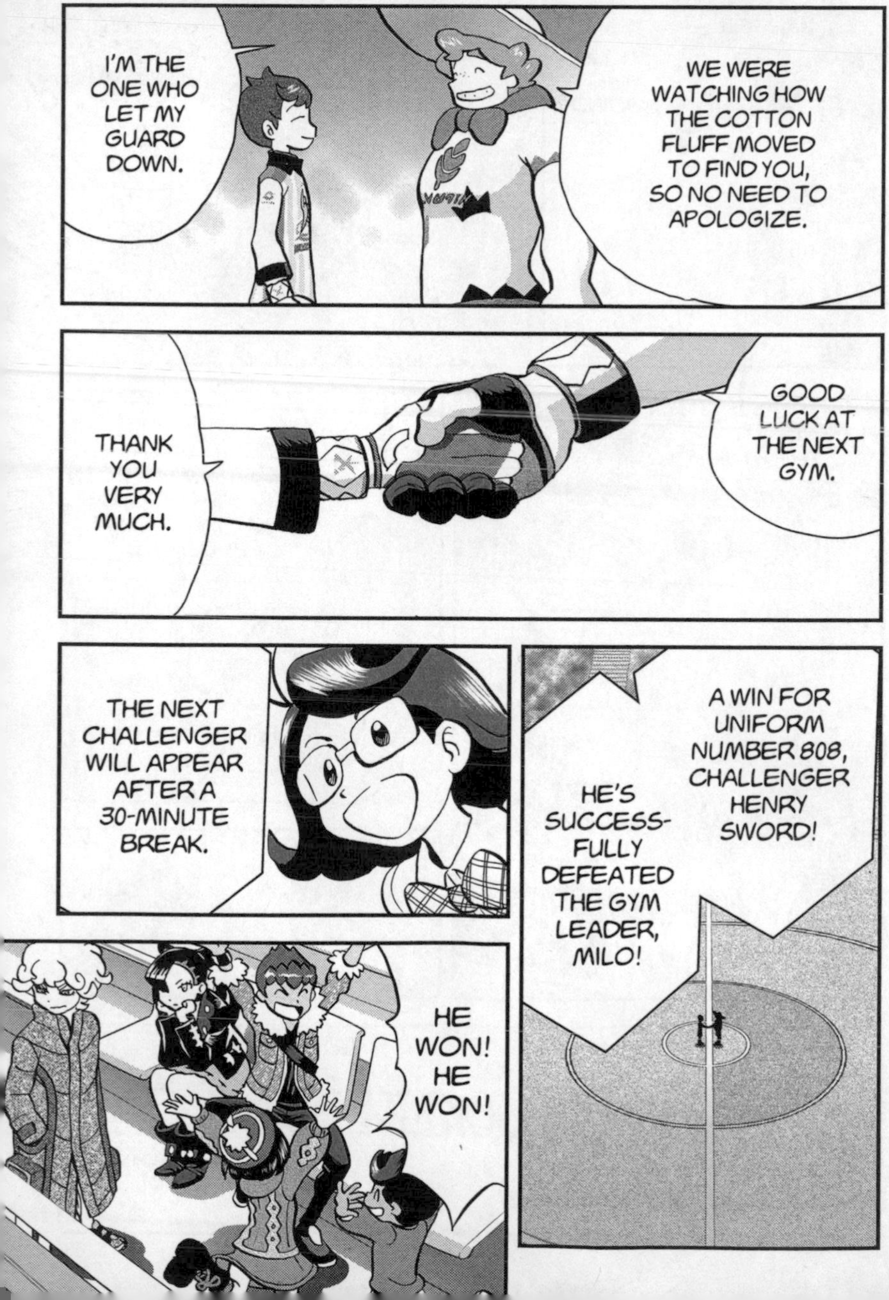
WE WERE WATCHING HOW THE COTTON FLUFF MOVED TO FIND YOU, SO NO NEED TO APOLOGIZE.
I'M THE ONE WHO LET MY GUARD DOWN.
GOOD LUCK AT THE NEXT GYM.
THANK YOU VERY MUCH.
A WIN FOR UNIFORM NUMBER 808, CHALLENGER HENRY SWORD!
HE'S SUCCESS-FULLY DEFEATED THE GYM LEADER, MILO!
THE NEXT CHALLENGER WILL APPEAR AFTER A 30-MINUTE BREAK.
HE WON! HE WON!

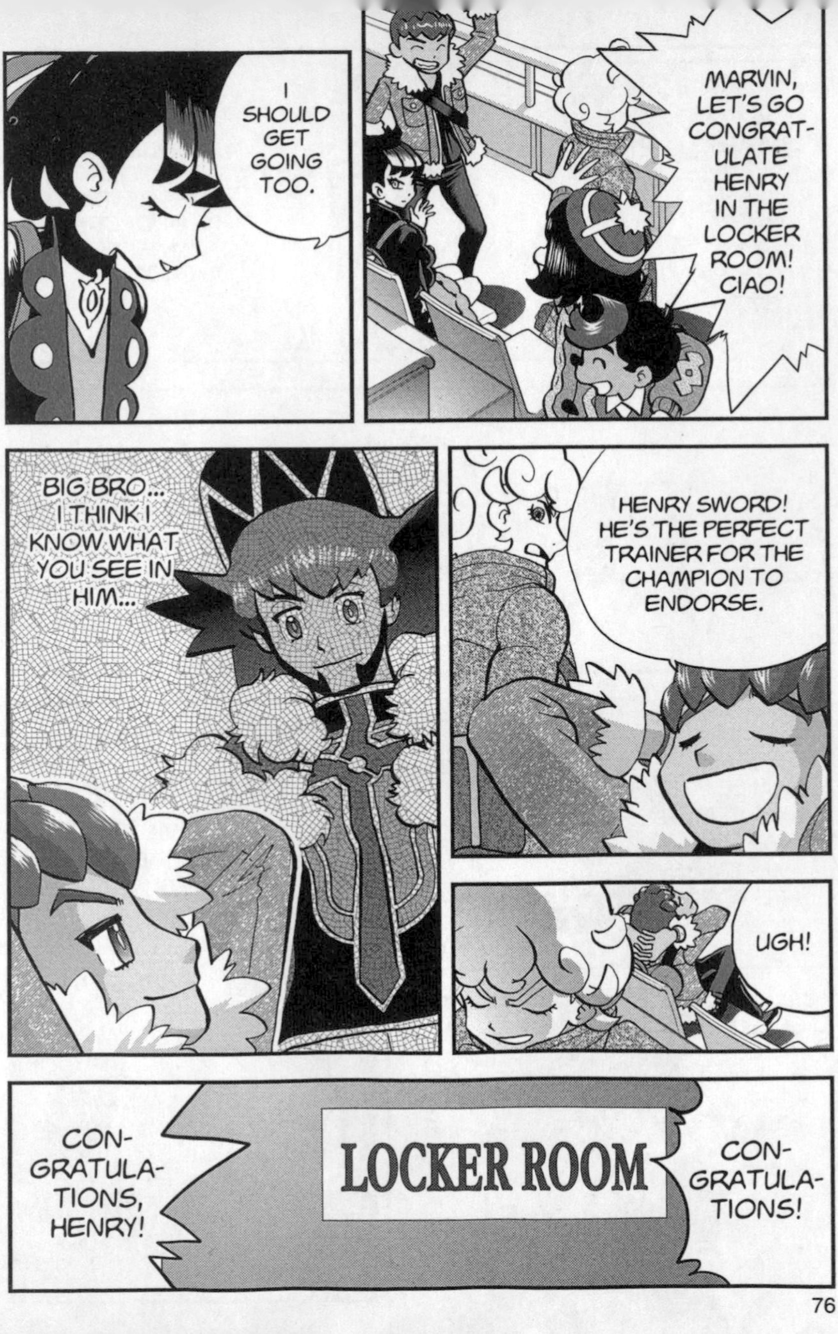
MARVIN, LET'S GO CONGRAT-ULATE HENRY IN THE LOCKER ROOM! CIAO!
I SHOULD GET GOING TOO.
HENRY SWORD! HE'S THE PERFECT TRAINER FOR THE CHAMPION TO ENDORSE.
UGH!
BIG BRO... I THINK I KNOW WHAT YOU SEE IN HIM...
CON-GRATULA-TIONS!
LOCKER ROOM
CON-GRATULA-TIONS, HENRY!

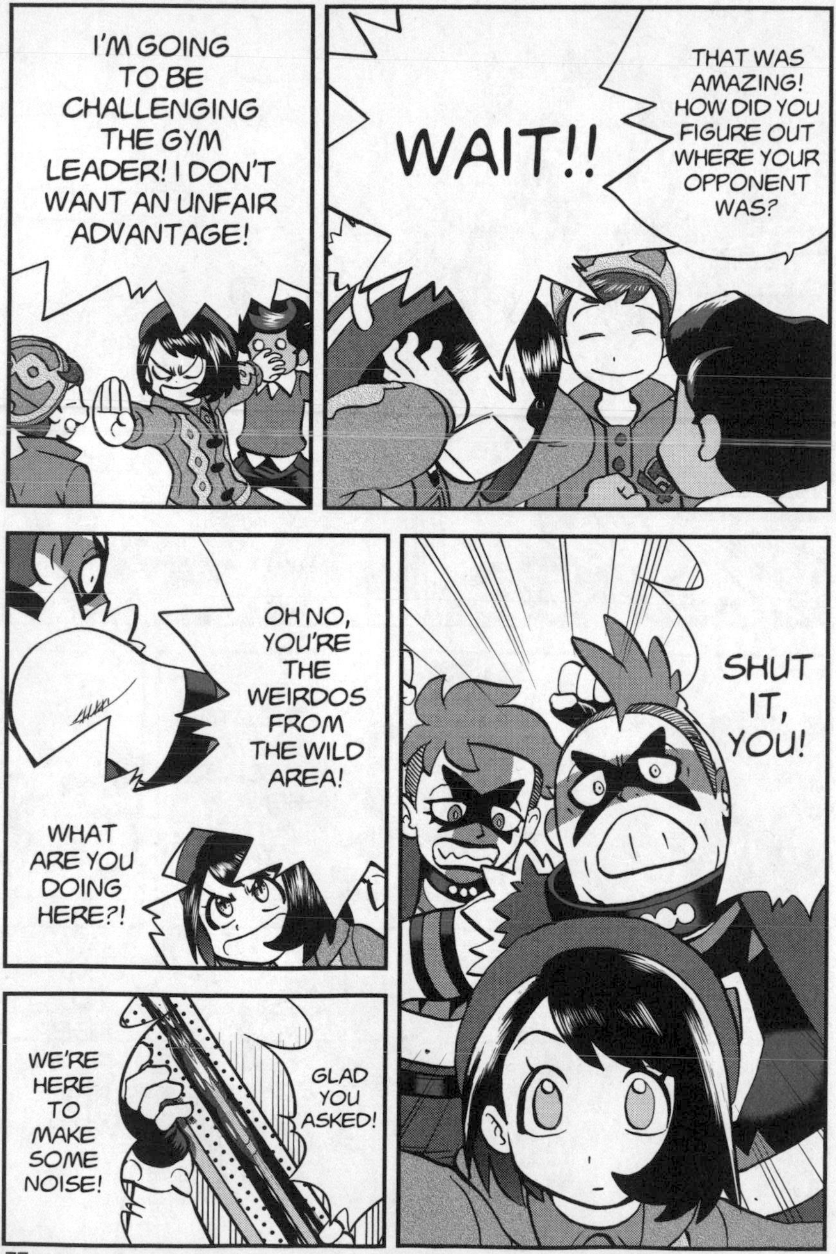
THAT WAS AMAZING! HOW DID YOU FIGURE OUT WHERE YOUR OPPONENT WAS?
WAIT!!
I'M GOING TO BE CHALLENGING THE GYM LEADER! I DON'T WANT AN UNFAIR ADVANTAGE!
SHUT IT, YOU!
OH NO, YOU'RE THE WEIRDOS FROM THE WILD AREA!
WHAT ARE YOU DOING HERE?!
GLAD YOU ASKED!
WE'RE HERE TO MAKE SOME NOISE!

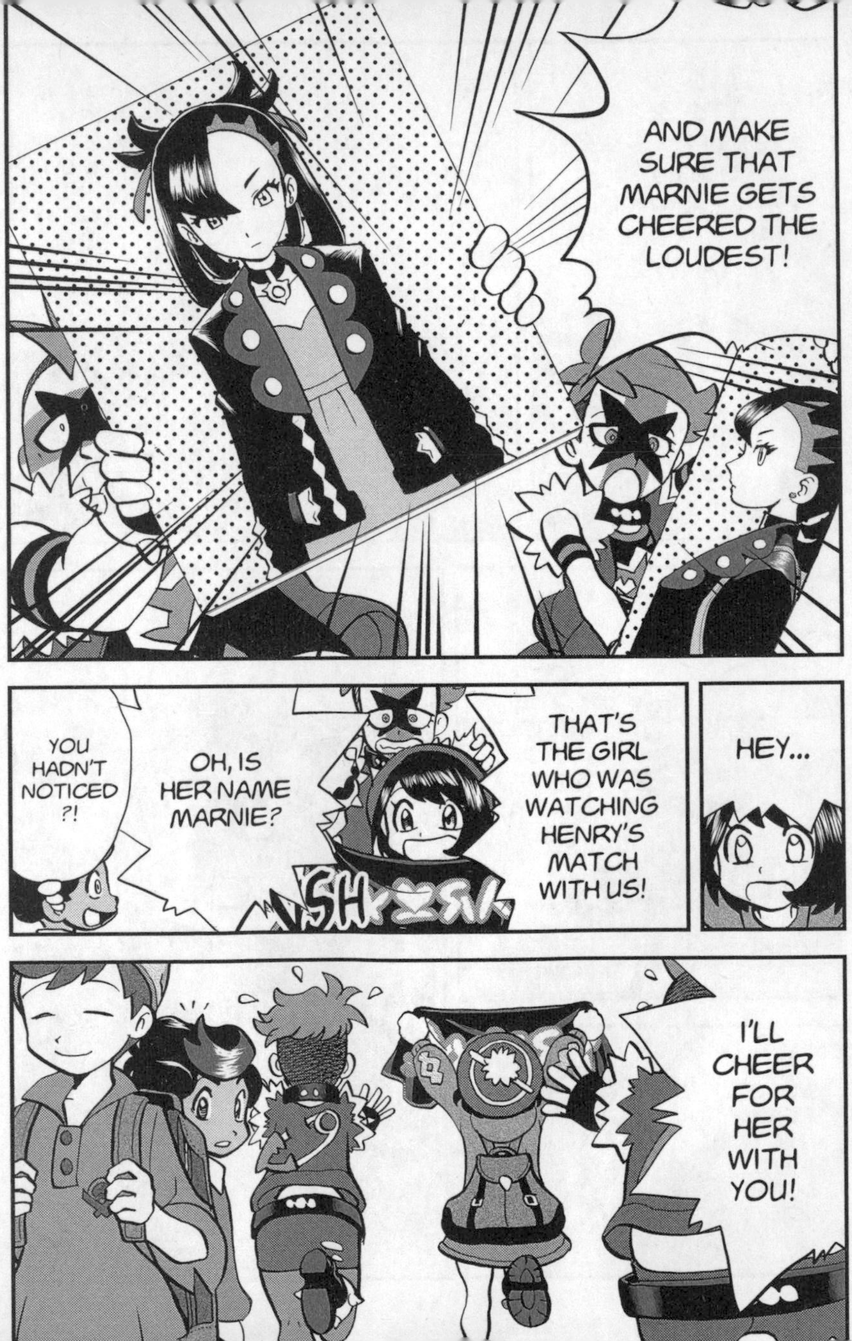
AND MAKE SURE THAT MARNIE GETS CHEERED THE LOUDEST!
HEY...
THAT'S THE GIRL WHO WAS WATCHING HENRY'S MATCH WITH US!
OH, IS HER NAME MARNIE?
YOU HADN'T NOTICED ?!
I'LL CHEER FOR HER WITH YOU!

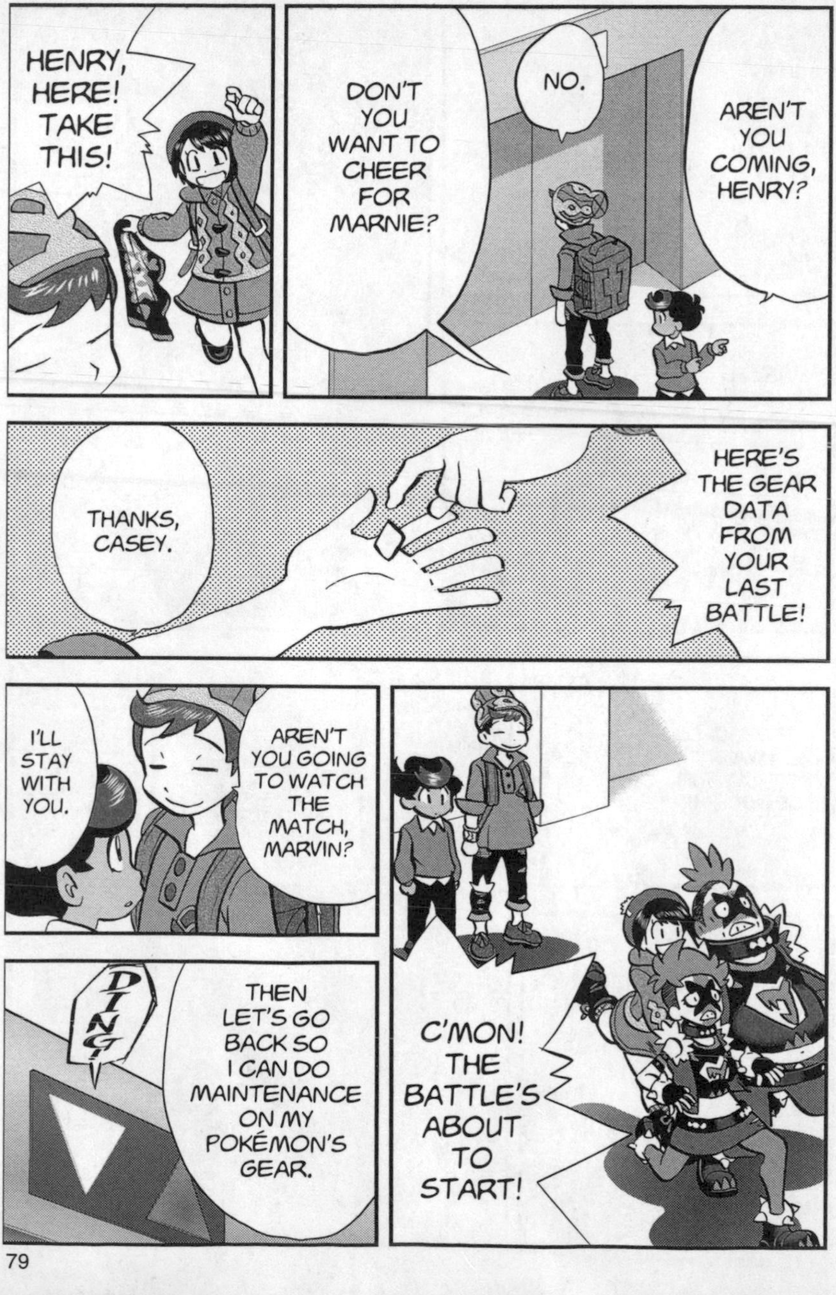
AREN'T YOU COMING, HENRY?
NO.
DON'T YOU WANT TO CHEER FOR MARNIE?
HENRY, HERE! TAKE THIS!
HERE'S THE GEAR DATA FROM YOUR LAST BATTLE!
THANKS, CASEY.
C'MON! THE BATTLE'S ABOUT TO START!
AREN'T YOU GOING TO WATCH THE MATCH, MARVIN?
I'LL STAY WITH YOU.
THEN LET'S GO BACK SO I CAN DO MAINTENANCE ON MY POKÉMON'S GEAR.
DING!

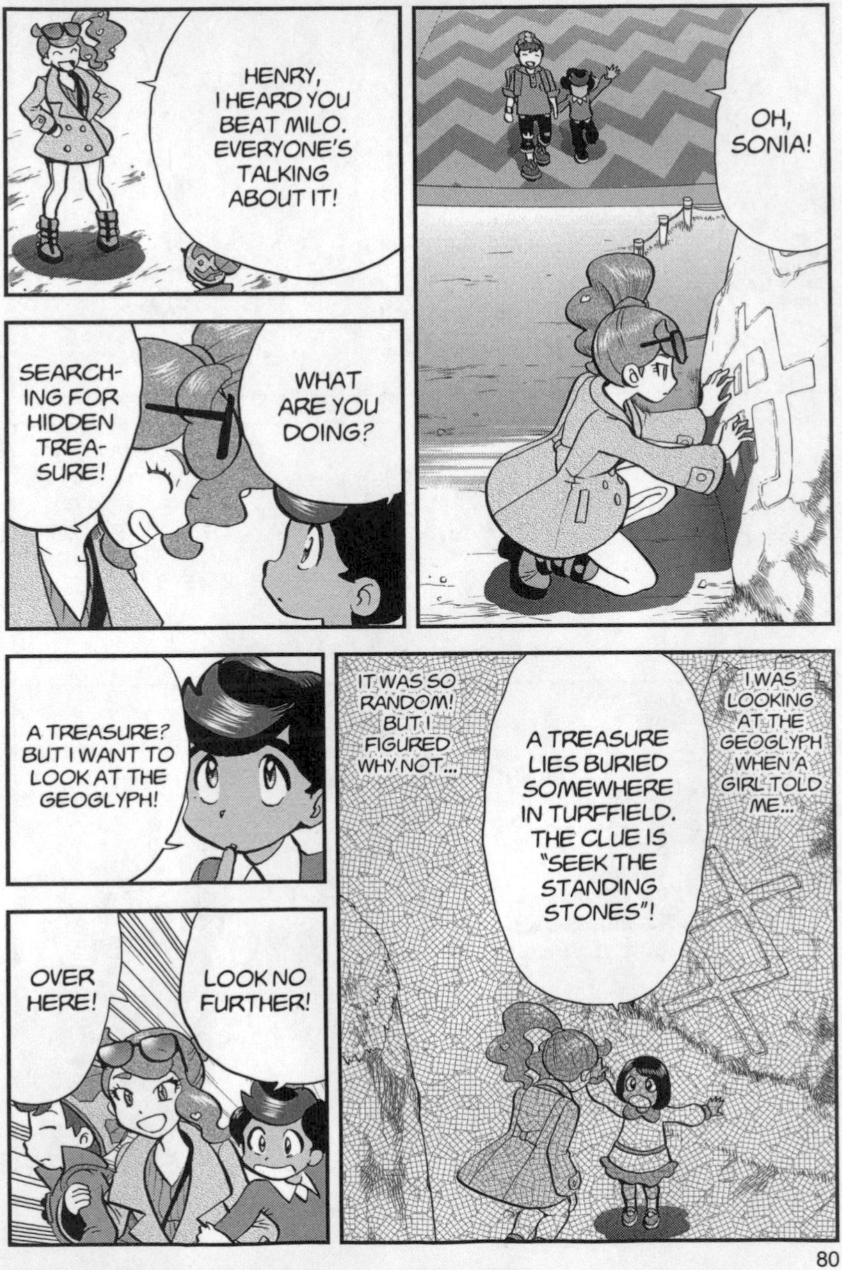
OH, SONIA!
HENRY, I HEARD YOU BEAT MILO. EVERYONE'S TALKING ABOUT IT!
WHAT ARE YOU DOING?
SEARCHING FOR HIDDEN TREASURE!
I WAS LOOKING AT THE GEOGLYPH WHEN A GIRL TOLD ME...
A TREASURE LIES BURIED SOMEWHERE IN TURFFIELD. THE CLUE IS "SEEK THE STANDING STONES"!
IT WAS SO RANDOM! BUT I FIGURED WHY NOT...
A TREASURE? BUT I WANT TO LOOK AT THE GEOGLYPH!
LOOK NO FURTHER!
OVER HERE!

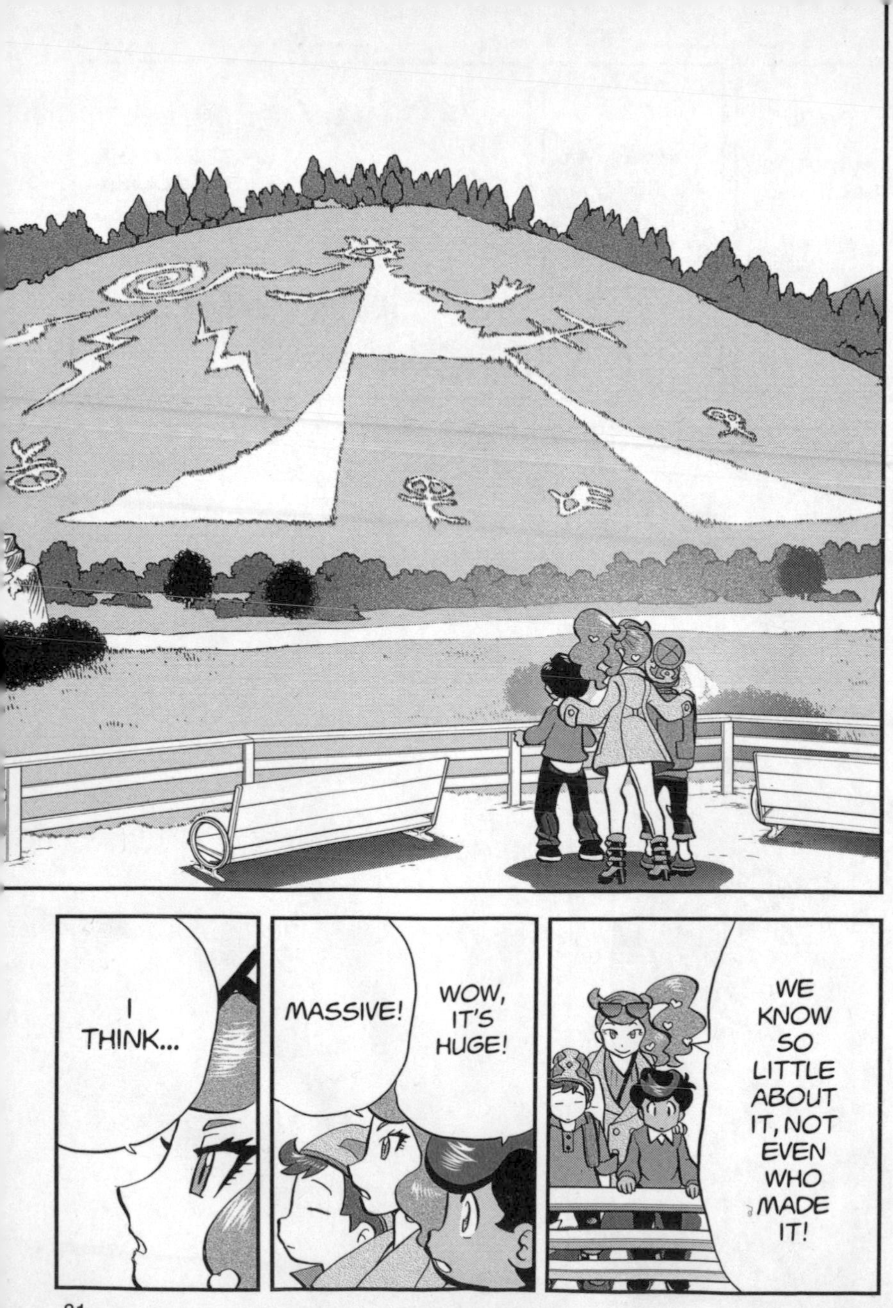
WE KNOW SO LITTLE ABOUT IT, NOT EVEN WHO MADE IT!
WOW, IT'S HUGE!
MASSIVE!
I THINK...

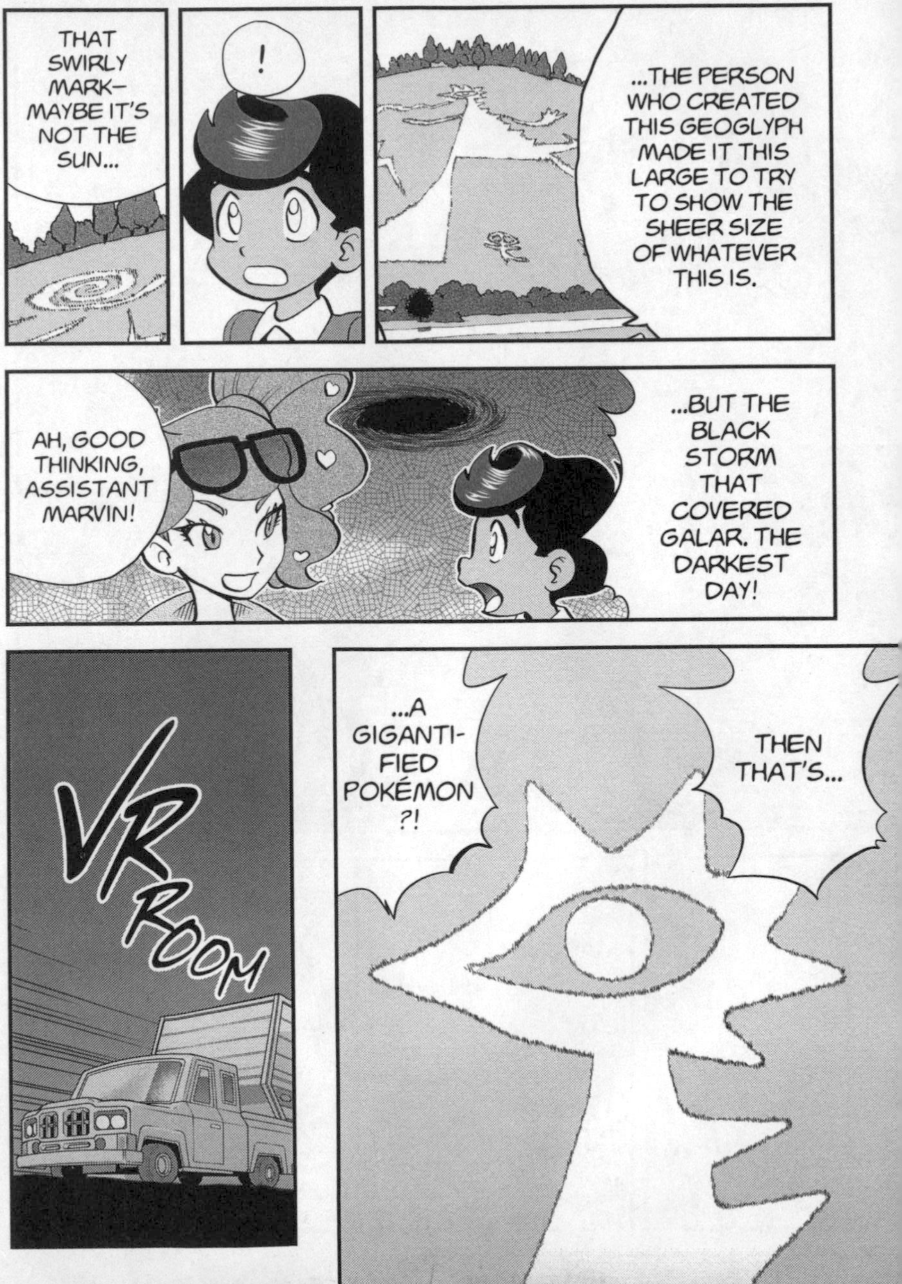
...THE PERSON WHO CREATED THIS GEOGLYPH MADE IT THIS LARGE TO TRY TO SHOW THE SHEER SIZE OF WHATEVER THIS IS.
!
THAT SWIRLY MARK—MAYBE IT'S NOT THE SUN...
...BUT THE BLACK STORM THAT COVERED GALAR. THE DARKEST DAY!
AH, GOOD THINKING, ASSISTANT MARVIN!
THEN THAT'S...
...A GIGANTIFIED POKÉMON ?!
VRROOM

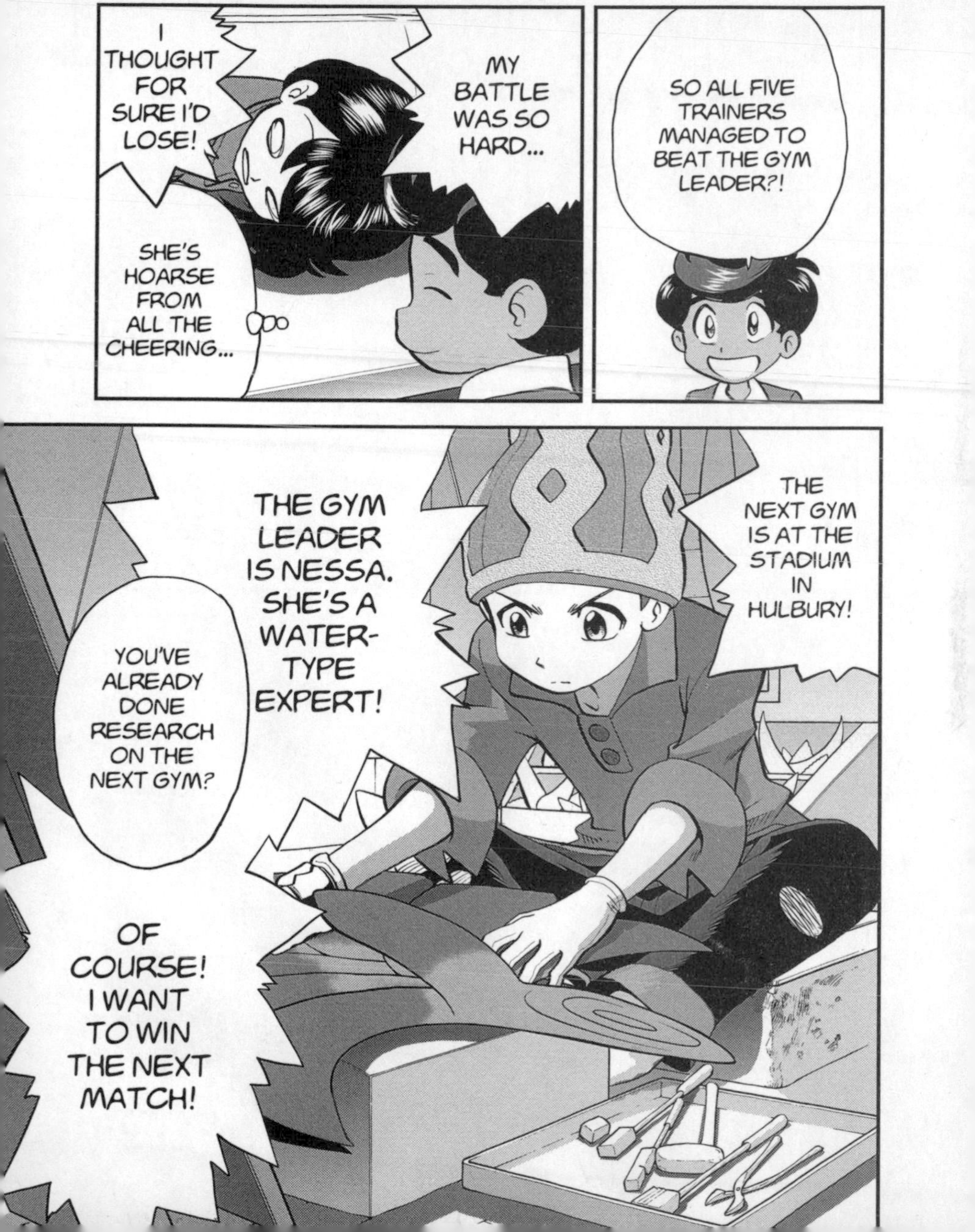
SO ALL FIVE TRAINERS MANAGED TO BEAT THE GYM LEADER?!
MY BATTLE WAS SO HARD...
I THOUGHT FOR SURE I'D LOSE!
SHE'S HOARSE FROM ALL THE CHEERING...
THE NEXT GYM IS AT THE STADIUM IN HULBURY!
THE GYM LEADER IS NESSA. SHE'S A WATER-TYPE EXPERT!
YOU'VE ALREADY DONE RESEARCH ON THE NEXT GYM?
OF COURSE! I WANT TO WIN THE NEXT MATCH!

Pokémon™

Sword & Shield

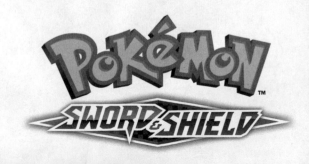

Henry Sword • Pokémon Data

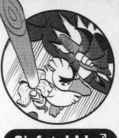

Lancelot

LV. 28

Sirfetch'd ♂

●GEAR:
LEEK SPEAR

HENRY'S FAVORITE POKÉMON. HENRY ALWAYS TAKES CARE OF ITS SPEAR, SO IT'S ALWAYS SHARP AND STRONG. IT USED TO BE A GALARIAN FARFETCH'D AND EVOLVED INTO ITS CURRENT FORM WHILE TRAINING.

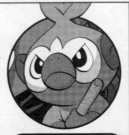

Twiggy

LV. 15

Grookey ♂

●GEAR:
DRUMSTICK

PROFESSOR MAGNOLIA ENTRUSTED THIS CHIMP POKÉMON TO HENRY. IT USES ITS DRUMSTICK TO STRIKE UP A BEAT AND ATTACK WITH SOUND WAVES. WHEN IT'S NOT FIGHTING, GROOKEY KEEPS ITS STICK IN ITS FUR.

Steeler

LV. 25

Gurdurr ♂

●GEAR:
STEEL BEAM

THIS GURDURR WAS THE FIRST DYNAMAX POKÉMON HENRY FACED AT THE WILD AREA. HENRY DESPERATELY WANTED TO CAPTURE THIS POKÉMON AND WAS HAPPY TO ADD IT TO HIS TEAM.

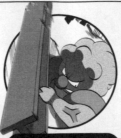

(What Is Gear?)

MAROWAK'S BONE, SAMUROTT'S SEAMITAR AND DELPHOX'S WAND ARE ALL EXAMPLES OF GEAR, THE WEAPONS AND ARMOR THAT POKÉMON USE IN THEIR BATTLES. HENRY'S DREAM IS TO BECOME AN EXPERT AT MAINTAINING POKÉMON GEAR. HE IS PARTICIPATING IN THE GYM CHALLENGE TO SEE IF HIS REFINED GEAR IS MORE EFFECTIVE IN BATTLE.

I SEE IT!
A BLURRY IMAGE OF SOMETHING THAT LOOKS LIKE A SWORD AND A SHIELD!

▲ HENRY RECALLS HIS EXPERIENCE AT THE SLUMBERING WEALD. COULD THESE BE GEAR?

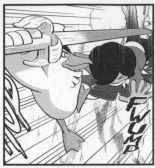

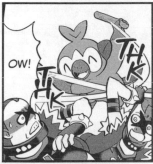

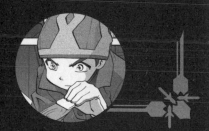

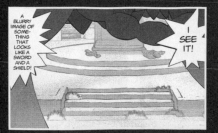

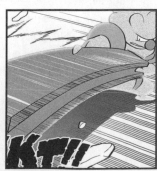

FWUMP

▲ IT HELPED SAVE MARVIN!

THK
OW!
THK

▲ EVEN THE TEAM YELL GRUNTS ARE STARTLED BY IT!

KT!!

▲ IT CAN SWING ITS STEEL BEAM AROUND POWERFULLY!

Hidenori Kusaka is the writer for *Pokémon Adventures*. Running continuously for over 20 years, *Pokémon Adventures* is the only manga series to completely cover all the *Pokémon* games and has become one of the most popular series of all time. In addition to writing manga, he also edits children's books and plans mixed-media projects for Shogakukan's children's magazines. He uses the Pokémon Electrode as his author portrait.

———————

Satoshi Yamamoto is the artist for *Pokémon Adventures*, which he began working on in 2001, starting with volume 10. Yamamoto launched his manga career in 1993 with the horror-action title *Kimen Senshi*, which ran in Shogakukan's *Weekly Shonen Sunday* magazine, followed by the series *Kaze no Denshosha*. Yamamoto's favorite manga creators/artists include Fujiko Fujio (*Doraemon*), Yukinobu Hoshino (*2001 Nights*) and Katsuhiro Otomo (*Akira*). He loves films, monsters, detective novels and punk rock music. He uses the Pokémon Swalot as his artist portrait.

Pokémon: Sword & Shield
Volume 2
VIZ Media Edition

Story by HIDENORI KUSAKA
Art by SATOSHI YAMAMOTO

©2021 Pokémon.
© 1995–2020 Nintendo / Creatures Inc. / GAME FREAK inc.
TM, ®, and character names are trademarks of Nintendo.
POCKET MONSTERS SPECIAL SWORD SHIELD Vol. 1
by Hidenori KUSAKA, Satoshi YAMAMOTO
© 2020 Hidenori KUSAKA, Satoshi YAMAMOTO
All rights reserved.
Original Japanese edition published by SHOGAKUKAN.
English translation rights in the United States of America, Canada, the United Kingdom,
Ireland, Australia and New Zealand arranged with SHOGAKUKAN.

Original Cover Design—Hiroyuki KAWASOME (grafio)

Translation—Tetsuichiro Miyaki
English Adaptation—Molly Tanzer
Touch-Up & Lettering—Annaliese "Ace" Christman
Cover Color — Philana Chen
Design—Alice Lewis
Editor—Joel Enos

The stories, characters and incidents mentioned
in this publication are entirely fictional.

Printed in the U.S.A.

Published by VIZ Media, LLC
P.O. Box 77010
San Francisco, CA 94107

10 9 8 7 6 5 4 3 2 1
First printing, December 2021

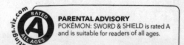

PARENTAL ADVISORY
POKÉMON: SWORD & SHIELD is rated A
and is suitable for readers of all ages.

viz.com

Coming Next Volume

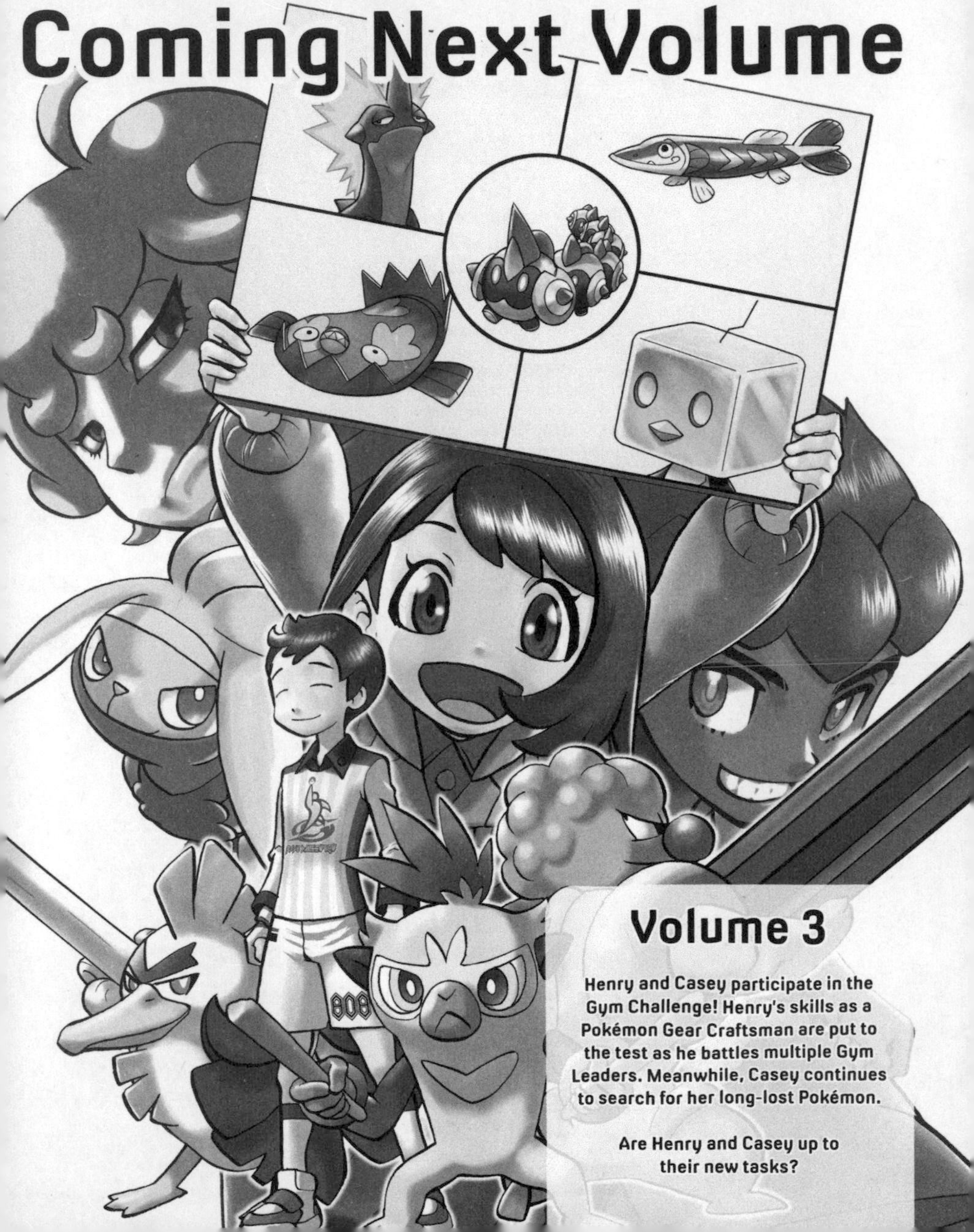

Volume 3

Henry and Casey participate in the Gym Challenge! Henry's skills as a Pokémon Gear Craftsman are put to the test as he battles multiple Gym Leaders. Meanwhile, Casey continues to search for her long-lost Pokémon.

Are Henry and Casey up to their new tasks?

Story
Hidenori Kusaka

Art
Satoshi Yamamoto

Sun dreams of money. Moon dreams of
scientific discoveries. When their paths cross
with Team Skull, both their plans go awry...

**PICK UP YOUR COPY AT YOUR
LOCAL BOOK STORE.**

POCKET COMICS

STORY & ART BY **SANTA HARUKAZE**

BLACK & WHITE

LEGENDARY POKÉMON

X•Y

A Pokémon pocket-sized book chock-full of four-panel gags, Pokémon trivia and fun quizzes based on the characters you know and love!

www.viz.com

POKÉMON ADVENTURES 20TH ANNIVERSARY ILLUSTRATION BOOK

THE ART OF

STORY AND ART BY
Satoshi Yamamoto

A collection of beautiful full-color art from the artist of the Pokémon Adventures graphic novel series! In addition to illustrations of your favorite Pokémon, this vibrant volume includes exclusive sketches and storyboards, four pull-out posters, and an exclusive manga side story!

Pokémon

MEWTWO STRIKES BACK
EVOLUTION

Story and Art by **Machito Gomi**

Original Concept by Satoshi Tajiri
Supervised by Tsunekazu Ishihara
Script by Takeshi Shudo

A manga adventure inspired by the hit Pokémon movie!

VIZ

Akira's summer vacation in the Alola region heats up when he befriends a Rockruff with a mysterious gemstone. Together, Akira hopes they can achieve his newfound dream of becoming a Pokémon Trainer and master the amazing Z-Move. But first, Akira needs to pass a test to earn a Trainer Passport. This becomes more difficult when Rockruff gets kidnapped! And then Team Kings shows up with—you guessed it—evil plans for world domination!

Story & Art
TENYA YABUNO

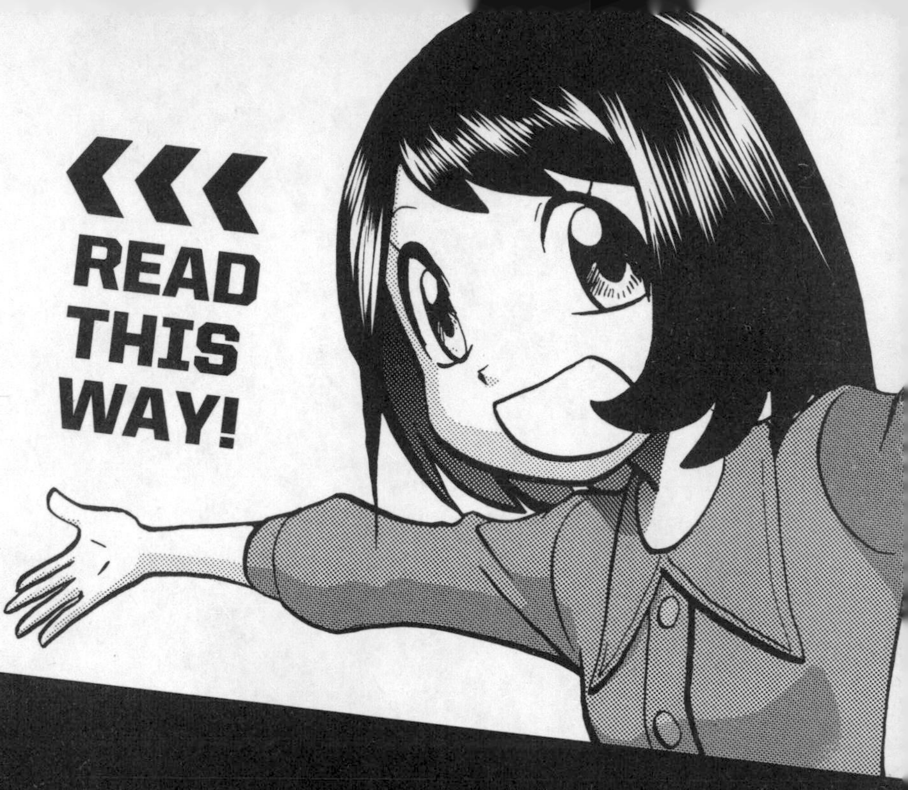
READ THIS WAY!

THIS IS THE END OF THIS GRAPHIC NOVEL!

To properly enjoy this VIZ Media graphic novel, please turn it around and begin reading from right to left.

This book has been printed in the original Japanese format in order to preserve the orientation of the original artwork. Have fun with it!

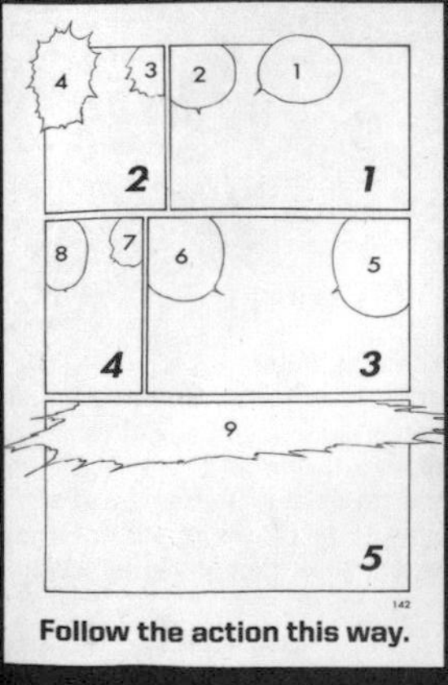
1
2
3
4
5
6
7
8
9
1
2
3
4
5

Follow the action this way.